ROCKET GIRLS

THE LAST PLANET

HOUSUKE NOJIRI

ROCKET GIRLS
THE LAST PLANET

HOUSUKE NOJIRI

TRANSLATED BY ALEXANDER O. SMITH

HAIKA SORU

SAN FRANCISCO

Rocket Girls 2
© 1996 Housuke Nojiri
First published in Japan in 1996 by Fujimishobo Co., Ltd., Tokyo.
English translation rights arranged by KADOKAWA SHOTEN Co., Ltd., Tokyo.

English translation © 2011 VIZ Media, LLC
Cover art by Katsuya Terada

HAIKASORU
Published by
VIZ Media, LLC
295 Bay Street
San Francisco, CA 94133

www.haikasoru.com

Library of Congress Cataloging-in-Publication Data

Nojiri, Hosuke, 1961-
  [Tenshi wa kekka orai. English]
  Rocket girls : the last planet / Housuke Nojiri ; translated by Alexander O. Smith.
     p. cm.
  ISBN 978-1-4215-3765-8
  I. Title.
  PL873.5.O52T4613 2011
  895.6'36--dc22
                            2010053691

The rights of the author of the work in this publication to be so identified have been asserted
in accordance with the Copyright, Designs and Patents Act 1988. A CIP catalogue record
for this book is available from the British Library.

Printed in the U.S.A.
First printing, March 2011

CONTENTS

CHAPTER ONE

HOMECOMING

[ACT 1]

"HEEEEY, EVERYBODY! It's me, from Fujimi TV, Keiko-on-the-beat, your favorite reporter-on-the-street! *Don't* touch that remote!

"We've come all the way to the Solomon Space Center here in the South Pacific on the trail of everyone's favorite astronauts, Yukari Morita and Matsuri! And what hotties—er, astronauts they are!

"I know what you're thinking: 'South Pacific? That's like right next door compared to *space*,' but believe me, it's a lot tougher getting *here* than getting up *there*. We're talking trains, planes, boats…three days in all! Our crew is pooped, but we're not going to let that get between us and the story.

"And let's not forget that Yukari came here all by herself during her sophomore-year summer vacation! Pretty impressive. And chasing after her long-lost father? It doesn't tug on the heart strings any more than that, folks.

"That's right, she was searching for her father, but she found so much more here at the Solomon Space Center. You might even call it *destiny*.

9

"It takes a lot to make an astronaut, and this little girl—who, by the way, dropped out of, oh, only the *most famous girls' school in Yokohama*, Nellis Academy, to devote her life to space—is no exception. Incredible!

"And then there's Yukari's half sister and backup crew, Matsuri. Raised among the local Taliho as one of their own, she's a budding shaman *and* an astronaut. Not every day you meet one of those!

"This is the fourth installment of our special report on these girls, and we've got something *really* special for you today. That's right, a broadcast *live* from space! Yukari, you read me? I just love saying that! Oh, Yukaaaaari?"

The fingernails-on-chalkboard reportage hopped through three land-based transmitters and two satellites and returned, bringing back a picture of...empty space.

"Huh? Are we live?" said a disembodied voice from off-camera. The picture swooped until its wide-angle lens showed the sea. Nothing but sea from the bottom of the screen to the arc of the horizon near the middle.

The camera tilted, and a girl in a white, skintight space suit appeared from the bottom of the screen. She was floating in space, a maneuvering gun in her right hand and a lifeline gripped tightly in the other.

The orbiter drifted into view by her feet. One of the hatches was open, revealing part of the pilot's seat assembly inside.

"Hello, Earth. This is the spaceship *Rambutan*, Captain Yukari Morita reporting."

Behind her visor, Yukari's eyes were wide open. She had something like a smirk on her face. "I'd like to introduce my copilot—"

Another hatch opened, and Matsuri Morita called out, "*Hoi!* It's me, Matsuri!" She waved, an exuberant grin on her tanned face. When Matsuri waved, it was a full-body affair. She shook like a dog wagging its tail.

Yukari gave a short blast with her gun to straighten herself to the plane of the picture. "The camera you're seeing me through is attached to a utility arm on the nose of the craft. What you see at the bottom—that is, toward my feet—is *Rambutan*'s hull. If you could see the whole thing, you'd notice it has an oval shape and is about the size of a sedan. It only seats two, so right now we're at maximum capacity. And, er..."

Yukari twisted, looking around behind her. "Right now we're approaching northwestern Africa, er...about three hundred kilometers over the Canary Islands. You can see the Straits of Gibraltar coming up. A little farther and we'll be able to see the Pyrenees and the Sahara at about the same time. Then we'll be over the Mediterranean and Syria, Iran, Iraq, and Saudi Arabia—I'm pretty sure there is at least one war going on down there right now."

"But not to worry!" Matsuri chimed in. "Director Kinoshita says we're totally out of Scud and Patriot missile range!"

Yukari grinned. "That's right! Let me put it in perspective for you: if we were flying as high as, say, eye-level, a Scud would have a hard time getting even as high as my knees."

What the hell are they babbling about? Nasuda frowned where he stood in the center guestroom. A single pane of glass divided him from the main floor of the control center. *Just stick to the program, ladies.* If they said anything about the surface, it should be the usual "From up here, there are no national boundaries." Period.

"There are some people who compare our rockets to missiles, but frankly, we've got ballistic missiles whipped in terms of altitude and speed, so good luck hitting us..." Yukari's voice trailed off as common sense finally caught up with her. "Let's get back to the ship and see how those goldfish are doing, shall we? One moment—"

Yukari went inside and the camera switched to an internal monitor.

Matsuri could be seen sitting on the left as Yukari came drifting into the orbiter to take the seat on the right. Once both hatches were closed, Yukari's hand reached down toward the bottom of the frame and she began to adjust something off-camera.

The two girls removed their helmets. Both of them had long hair, Yukari's in braids on either side of her face and Matsuri's in a ponytail down her back.

"There—now where were we," Yukari said, brushing her bangs out of her eyes. "Right, the goldfish. They're in this container-thingy..."

The inside of the orbiter was small, about the size of a pickup-truck cabin. Yukari bumped into the wall several times as she moved to a new position lying across Matsuri's knees.

"Er, I know this isn't exactly the graceful weightlessness of space that you might have been expecting, but as you can see, it's rather cramped inside the orbiter—"

Yukari fiddled with a panel on the side of a shock-absorbing chair, molded to precisely fit the curve of Yukari's spine. The back of the chair fell forward, revealing a storage rack filled with test equipment.

"This is the testing array for the goldfish. It's very compact. The fish tank is on the upper level, here. There's a monitoring and recording device in the middle, and the power and environmental support are near the bottom. Now for the fishies."

Yukari pulled out the fish container and yanked the CCD camera from its Velcro anchor on the instrument panel to give the viewers a close-up. "This tank is only about the size of a lunchbox, but it holds twenty-four goldfish!" She looked at the fish. "They really pack you in like sardines—no offense, guys." She looked back at the camera. "If we just left them in there, they'd run out of oxygen quickly, so we have to keep the water cycling. Can you make this out? They're all swimming nicely. Right after takeoff, all the poor things could do was spin around, but they seem to have gotten used to the low-G environment."

Yukari glanced down at her watch as she talked. Broadcast time was almost up.

"We'll be bringing these fish back with us when we come home. Our planned landing zone is in the deep water off the Seychelles Islands. From there, they'll travel by helicopter and plane until these guys are safely back at the Space Science Laboratory in Sagamihara. And...well, that's it for our broadcast. So long!"

The image of the two girls faded from the screen and the picture returned to the flight tracking chart. Nasuda glanced at the NASA bigwig next to him and inwardly breathed a sigh of relief. It hadn't been a total disaster. He wouldn't have understood the girls' Japanese, anyway. Overall, the sight of them up there actually doing things had probably been good PR.

"Well, Director Holden, what do you think?" Nasuda smiled. "As you can see, we are well past the testing stage with our manned flights here at the SSA."

"Impressive," Holden grunted, a sneer in his voice. "You pick two of the smallest girls you could find—small even for Japanese—and specially design the orbiter to cram them in. *Very* impressive."

"That may be the impression our detractors would like you to have—"

Holden turned and glared at him. "Oh, it's public knowledge, Director."

"But what space vessel *isn't* constructed with the utmost attention to reducing load? We are not in the freight transportation business. Our one and only objective is to get people into space at the absolute minimum cost. The cost of lifting that two-seat orbiter once is only two billion yen—one fifteenth of the cost to launch one of your space shuttles."

Holden shrugged as if to indicate he already knew this.

"If the SSA were to participate in the construction of your

planned space station," Nasuda continued, "you'd realize a considerable reduction in both cost and time. You could use the leftover funds as you wished."

"I'm not as concerned about cost as I am about risk," the NASA director replied. "I'll be frank. Your SSA has only been sending up manned flights for half a year now. Your astronauts are charming little angels, to be sure, but you're asking for a great deal of courage if you want me to place the fate of the International Space Station in the hands of two teenagers."

"I understand your trepidation, of course. That's why I want you to take this opportunity to see just what we're doing in space—to remove any misconceptions you might have."

Holden frowned. "You doing another broadcast?"

"Only one more. While we're preparing for that, I'll show you around our manufacturing facility. I'm sure you'd like to see our solid fuel system. It's not every fuel that can produce a relative thrust of three hundred twenty..."

"Aaaaa—urp!"

Yukari swallowed a yawn. It had been twenty-two hours since launch. She had taken naps in shifts with Matsuri, but with nothing to do besides the broadcast, being in orbit was pretty boring.

Three hours till we land.

It was time.

Yukari had refrained from taking any solids—there were no toilet facilities in the capsule, which could make things really uncomfortable—but some things were worth the risk.

"We have time until the next broadcast, right?"

"*Hoi?*"

Yukari pulled a duralumin case out from beneath her shock-absorption chair. Bringing personal items on board the capsule had been strictly forbidden, but claiming "womanly needs," Yukari had managed to win this one small concession. The case was small, and its weight limited, but the contents were entirely her responsibility and most importantly, not subject to screening.

She opened the case to reveal an assortment of carefully wrapped dim sum.

"Ta-da! Shrimp dumplings, courtesy of Tianjin Restaurant. Tasty even when chilled."

Matsuri's usually cheerful face broke into an even bigger smile. "Good call!"

Yukari laughed. "You know it. I had Hanrei make one of her special midnight deliveries."

Yukari seized one of the dumplings and crammed it into her mouth. Zero gravity made everything taste bland, but after suffering through a regimen of carefully portioned, utterly flavorless lumps of protein, the oily, shrimp-filled dough balls were deeply satisfying.

"*Mmph*, smell that shrimp! C'mon, Matsuri, you have some."

"Any vinegar soy sauce?"

"Now don't get greedy. You know how hard it was sneaking these in here?"

"I thought as much," Matsuri said, shaking her head, "which is why I brought this." Matsuri reached under her own seat and pulled out a case, which she opened to reveal a tube of vinegar soy sauce.

Yukari gaped at her. "When did you—"

"There's more!" Matsuri grinned, turning the case to show Yukari. "Let's see. Mayonnaise, ketchup, mustard...all here!"

"Hey, you keep those away from my dumplings!"

Matsuri loved condiments, the more garishly colored and artificially flavored the better. Her condiment tool kit could turn the finest cuisine into junk food. Other than her flight training, this was the only aspect of Yukari's culture that Matsuri had fully embraced.

"Oh wait, there's one more thing."

"It better not be relish."

"Dessert!" Matsuri crouched down and opened the storage

space beneath their life raft. "Did you know there's a dead space beneath here?"

"Don't they check that before launch?"

"Oh, I asked the spirits to hide it so they wouldn't find it."

"Um...okay?"

Yukari's eyes went wide when she saw the giant, spike-festooned tropical fruit in Matsuri's hand.

"A durian?"

"I found one growing in the jungle off to the side of the runway the other day." Matsuri reached up with her hand, retrieving the survival knife from a hatch above their heads.

"Wait, Matsuri, you know how bad those things reek—"

Oh, but they *were* delicious. Some people made special trips to the tropics just to eat durian. The smell, however, was appropriately likened to a pool of rancid custard sitting in a sewer.

"Ooh. Perfectly ripe!" Matsuri held the durian between her knees and sank the knife into it.

"Waah! Stop! Stop! You'll stink the whole place up!" Yukari reached out and grabbed Matsuri's hand holding the knife.

"*Hoi?* What's wrong?"

When Yukari moved, the case had drifted off her lap. Then, when she grabbed Matsuri's hand, her knee had gone up, scoring a direct hit on the bottom of Matsuri's case and sending its contents flying—a Big Bang of shrimp dumplings and vinegar soy sauce.

"Whee! That's cool!"

"It's totally *not* cool! We have to clean this up!"

"Look, Yukari, you can scoop it out of the air with your mouth! Yummy!"

"Would you stop eating and start grabbing those dumplings! If we don't hurry—"

Director Holden stared at the screen in stunned silence.

The wide-angle lens of the camera showed the entire capsule in unforgiving clarity. Dumplings and droplets of vinegar soy sauce and the durian swam around, like a slow-motion computer model of Brownian motion, sometimes colliding and fusing, only to separate again.

In the middle of it all were the two girls, shock on their faces, arms flailing.

"I'm uncomfortably put in mind of the *Apollo* 1 tragedy," the NASA director said to Nasuda. "So tell me. What else do your 'astronauts' do?"

[ACT 2]

TWO HOURS LATER, the orbiter entered its final orbit.

"Solomon, this is *Rambutan*. We're preparing for reentry."

"Roger that, orbiter. You finish collecting the loose objects?"

Yukari detected the faintest hint of sarcasm in Kinoshita's cool voice.

"All, er, objects have been collected…and all indicators are green. We're ready to come home."

"Roger that. Over and out."

"All right." Yukari glanced over at her copilot. "Let's nail this splashdown and win back some of the reputation we've just squandered. All's well that ends well, right?" She grinned. "Woo-hoo! Seychelles coral reefs, here I come!"

Yukari opened her landing checklist. "So, what's first? Helium pressure?"

"*Hoi*, HePRS, open!"

"Nitrogen supply?"

"N2SPLY, on!"

"Attitude adjustment…RCS-MAN." Yukari set the controls

to manual and began adjusting their attitude by hand. Once you got used to it, it was a lot faster than entering numbers with the sequencer. Control panels throughout the capsule began to chirp and blink as the orbiter rotated until its stern was facing forward.

"*Hoi*, we're in position."

"All right. Solomon, this is *Rambutan*. Standing by for reentry burn."

"*Rambutan*, you're cleared for reentry burn."

"Starting reentry burn sequence."

Yukari flipped up the sequencer start switch cover and placed her finger on the button.

Beep beep beep beep.

"*Hoi?* We're getting an error from the fish tank."

"Great, what now?" Yukari swore under her breath and undid her harness. Her body floated up into the cabin and she twisted until she was facing the control panel behind her seat. "Okay...so what's wrong?"

"*Rambutan*, this is Solomon. You have an error in your testing equipment?"

"*Hoi*, we do. Yukari's checking it out."

"We're putting a hold on reentry until it's fixed. Bringing those goldfish back alive is a success condition for your mission."

"We know, we know," Yukari snapped. "We're getting error code...115."

"Error code 115, roger. They'll look into it at Sagamihara. If we can get that fixed within twenty minutes, you can come home as planned. Otherwise we're going to our second splashdown target."

"No way! That's in the South China Sea! There's, like, pirates there!"

"If you don't like it, you'll just have to make those repairs in time. But don't rush it."

"Roger."

A communication came in from the Space Science Laboratory in Sagamihara almost immediately.

"*Rambutan*, this is Space Lab. According to our telemeter the error code is 315. Confirm."

"*Rambutan* to Space Lab, the panel's showing error code *one*-one-five, not *three*-one-five."

"Roger that. None of the device monitors are showing problems. Can you send us a video feed of the fish?"

"Our video channel's closed already. Should we assume this error's a glitch, then?"

"Hold on, we're still looking into it. We'll be with you shortly."

"Roger."

Yukari returned to her seat and awaited instructions. "Nine minutes…I was really looking forward to doing some skin diving."

"Space Lab to *Rambutan*. We have an IFM request for you. You're going to have to do some maintenance. First we need a visual check of the goldfish."

"Roger."

Yukari frowned and once again left her chair. "Sorry, Matsuri, we gotta hug again."

"*Hoi*."

She was submitting a design change request as soon as they got back. It was ridiculous to have to get out of her seat every time she wanted to do anything with the testing equipment.

Yukari slid over Matsuri, pushed down her seatback, and peered into the fish container. The goldfish were swimming erratically in every direction, which wasn't unusual, except that their mouths were opening and closing a little too fast.

"Space Lab, this is *Rambutan*. The goldfish are all alive, but they seem to be opening and closing their mouths more quickly than usual."

"How fast, exactly? Like, open…open…open?"

"No, more like open, open, open."

"Can you check the reading on the diffused oxygen monitor? Go to MON, press the up arrow twice, code 107."

"Roger that. MON, up arrow twice..."

"Yukari, did you hear that?"

"Hear what?"

Behind her, Matsuri shrugged. "I dunno. It sounded like a compression pump starting up."

"Could you be quiet a sec? I forgot the code!"

"Oops, sorry."

"Space Lab, could you give me that code again?"

"That's 107."

"Right, 107. The monitor's reading 0218."

"Yukari, the sequencer's started up."

"Huh?"

"*Rambutan*, the DO levels are too low. I want you to check the QD on the fish container."

"Roger that, Space Lab. What did you say, Matsuri?"

"I said the sequencer's going! It's going to start a burn soon!"

"But we didn't start the sequencer!"

"Then someone else did. Look at the SEQ display scroll by."

"No way!" Yukari's face went pale. It occurred to her that she had left the switch cover open. Had she accidentally bumped it when she was maneuvering around the cabin?

"Well we have to stop it right away!"

The shock of the burn came just as Matsuri was reaching for the instrument panel.

"Yipes!"

The experimentation panel hit Yukari's face at 0.1 G.

"Ow ow ow ow! Matsuri, cut off the OMS, now!"

"Your butt's in the way!"

Yukari grunted and twisted. "It's not *that* big. How about now?"

"Just a little farther."

"Will you stop that thing already!"

"There, got it!"

The sound of the compressor faded.

"*Rambutan*, this is Space Lab. Our telemetry's stopped. Is something wrong?"

"Oh, uh, well, I just ran into the panel. Maybe I accidentally turned the switch off with my nose—"

"*Rambutan*, this is Solomon. Our monitors are showing a brief OMS burn. What's going on up there?"

"Well, the sequencer just started up and—"

"Yukari," Matsuri whispered, "we're losing altitude."

"Could you read off the switch positions on panel one—"

"Wait. You stopped the burn manually—"

"This is Space Lab again. Once we have a signal can you resume your check of the QD—"

"That partial burn is problematic. Better prep for a crash landing—"

"Yukari! We're losing altitude fast!"

"Will you all just shut up for one second!" Yukari wailed. "I told them it was too much to do experiments and pilot this thing at the same time!"

Yukari had a laundry list of things she wanted to check with base, but their altitude had already fallen below 130 kilometers and the capsule was beginning to bump atmosphere. When the vivid orange plasma of reentry covered the windows, their radio would cease to function.

Yukari pushed all thoughts of the goldfish from her head and strapped herself in. Their angle of reentry was good. They'd make it into the atmosphere at least. But where would they land? Last estimates had put them somewhere between Northeast China, the Sea of Japan, the Japanese islands, and the North Pacific...

"Hope we don't land in North Korea," Yukari muttered, gritting her teeth against the rising gravity.

They were past 4 G now. It was becoming difficult to speak.

Six G. Yukari's body weighed six times more than it did at sea level, six times more than her bones and muscles were used to. The capsule vibrated like a saltshaker in the hands of an impatient child.

Yukari wondered for what seemed like the one-hundredth time why it always shook so much. She felt her body sinking into the seat until she felt like a human pancake, and she knew that the worst was yet to come.

[ACT 3]

ON A CONSOLE at the Ministry of Transportation Aircraft Traffic Control Center in Tokorozawa, a red light flashed.

"Chief! I got something here!"

The air controller in charge of Japan's central and northwest region stood up from his chair. "ID unknown...maybe a bad transmitter? It's going over the sea near Noto Penninsula at...Mach 11!"

The chief leaned over to look at the oval radar screen. A point of light was crossing it, headed straight for the Tokyo region at an incredible speed.

"No vessel name or identifying number? What's its altitude? Any secondary surveillance radar reading?"

"I'm not getting any response from the air-traffic control transponder. Nothing on audio, either. Think it's an American test flight? Didn't they have something called the Aurora—"

"What would a test flight be doing in our airspace? The SFD moving on this? Any word from Komatsu?"

"Haven't been able to get through to them."

"That better not be a North Korean missile."

"At that velocity we'll find out pretty damn soon if it is."

"The unidentified craft is over here now—in the West Kanto sector," the controller sitting at the station next to them called out. "It's heading for Tokyo, correct that, for Atsugi."

"Keep trying to contact Komatsu. Send all local flights for Narita and Haneda to Nagoya and Sendai. International flights can go to Osaka."

"Aircraft of unidentified nationality, this is Tokyo Control. Respond. Aircraft of unidentified nationality, respond immediately."

"The Komatsu airbase just scrambled its F-15s," the central Japan controller announced.

"Good luck catching that thing. Its speed is off the charts."

"Actually, it's decelerating. It's at Mach 3.2 now."

"Already? What *is* that thing?"

Just then, an unfamiliar voice came in on an emergency frequency.

"Uh...Mayday, Mayday. This is the spaceship *Rambutan*. Can anyone read me?"

"Spaceship?"

"Think it's some kind of prank?"

"Wait, what if it's those high school girls—"

"That's it. Answer them!"

"*Rambutan*, this is Tokyo Control. Give us your current altitude, rate of descent, and target destination."

"Our current altitude's 18.4 kilometers and we're coming down at about...two hundred twenty meters per second."

"Whaa—?" The flight controller gaped. "Eighteen point four kilometers, that's about...sixty thousand feet, okay. And the velocity's in meters per second, so, uh..."

Sweat beading on his forehead, the flight controller mashed the buttons on his calculator. Not only were the units totally different than the ones he was used to working with, but the numbers were higher by such a degree of magnitude his years of experience weren't doing him a bit of good. "Er, *Rambutan*, what's your splashdown target?"

"Our target was off the eastern coast of Africa, but we got the timing a bit wrong."

"Okay...so you missed Africa, and that's why you're here in Japan?" The controller shook his head. "Where are you headed right now?"

"I'd tell you if I knew. We're kind of in freefall here."

"Freefall? Wait, so—what?" Tossing his headset to the desktop, the controller began furiously scratching his head. "Chief! What the heck am I supposed to do with a spaceship?"

"Give me that." The chief grabbed the microphone. "*Rambutan*, you'll be in Atsugi Base airspace momentarily. I can't guarantee you won't be knocked out of the sky by a land-to-air missile."

"But Solomon should have contacted all the major airports and military bases!"

"We didn't hear anything."

"What about the other airports?"

"No idea. We are looking into it now."

"That won't be quick enough. Could you contact the U.S. military and the Japan Self-Defense Force for us?"

"Will do." The chief turned to the flight controller for central and northern Japan. "Get word to the U.S. military and the SDF right now. I don't care how you do it. Call every number you got."

"Right away."

"I'm not sure the Americans are going to like this much," one of the other controllers said.

"I'm sure they're already tracking her. And if they thought she was a missile, they'd have contacted us by now—or shot them down."

"*Rambutan* to Tokyo Control, we are at nine kilometers. We just deployed our main parachute. Our position is a little to the west of Tokyo, I think. Our GPS map isn't very detailed."

The flight control chief glanced at his radar screen. They had slowed to eight knots per hour.

"*Rambutan*, you're right over the city of Ayase, in Kanagawa Prefecture. I understand you can't control your descent?"

"Affirmative. We're dropping at about ten meters a second now. Hope we find some water to splashdown in."

"I'm not sure you will. You might even hit Yokohama. Want us to send out a rescue crew?"

"Yokohama..."

The voice over the speaker stopped abruptly. There was a brief moment of silence before Yukari spoke. "Yes, please. In Japan, I'm guessing that would be the police's jurisdiction?"

"I'm not sure we even have protocol for dealing with spacecraft, but I'll let the Kanagawa police know you're coming."

"Thank you."

"Good luck, *Rambutan*. Tokyo Control out."

Matsuri's eyes were glued to the periscope. The periscope tube ran through the middle of their instrument panel, down into the floor and through the hull, where it opened into a fish-eye lens.

"Whoa! Look at all the houses! I've never seen so many!"

"What about water? Can you see the ocean?"

"No. Oh, there it is. Pretty far off, though. Wow! What's that big tower?"

"Landmark Tower, by Yokohama harbor, probably."

"Aren't you from Yokohama, Yukari?"

"Actually, yeah."

Of all the places they could have crash-landed in the entire world, why Yokohama?

She hadn't even set foot on Japanese soil in ten months—and now she was about to leave a shallow crater in it.

"Will you stop gawking out the window and help me prep for splashdown?"

"*Hoi!* Where are we?"

"I need to switch power from the fuel cells to the shielded batteries and purge O_2 and H_2."

"Got it."

"Voltage normal. Okay, next cut off life support and get some ventilation going."

The air circulator for their life support system stopped and the smells of the greater Tokyo-Yokohama industrial area poured in through the vents.

Matsuri crinkled her nose. "Smells like the fuel factory on base."

"Smells like home."

They were only three hundred meters up now. Thirty seconds to the ground. Yukari took a look through the periscope.

No way are we making it to the ocean.

"Tokyo Control, this is *Rambutan*. We're below one thousand feet. Looks like we'll be crash-landing in the city."

"Roger that, *Rambutan*. We're tracking you on the high-res radar at Haneda. The police have a chopper en route. I think we've got you covered."

"Thanks for the help."

They'd be hitting the ground at ten meters per second—an impact they'd trained for. The problem was, what if they didn't hit open ground? There could be anything down there. High-voltage electrical lines, factories with hazardous materials, an expressway...

Yukari wrested her gaze from the outside and read the altitude gauge.

Two hundred meters.

"Is it just me, or have we been here before?" Yukari muttered.

"*Hoi?*"

One hundred meters.

"I mean, one time out of two, we're facing imminent death."

Fifty meters.

"No problem, Yukari, we'll be fine!"

Thirty meters.

"Today's a good day to die," Matsuri added.

"That's not what I'd call fine, Matsuri!"

The two girls braced for impact.

Zakooooosh.

There was a brief jolt as they hit the surface of something, sank a short distance, and came to rest. A water landing, amazingly enough. The only window on the orbiter was in the overhead hatch. Yukari looked through it and saw only sky.

She took a deep breath. "We made it?"

"We sure did!"

"Looks like we hit water."

"Looks like."

"Well, follow procedure. Inflate floats and release the dye marker."

The dye—an oily mixture that would float on the surface of the ocean—began spraying from the cone of the orbiter. A VHF/HF antenna extended at the same time as a buzzer began to sound in the cabin.

"System alert! Where is it?"

Yukari frantically scanned the instrumentation panel. There was a short in their preliminary power source. They were taking on water.

"Uh-oh, looks like we've sprung a leak!"

"*Hoi?* What do we do about that?"

Yukari looked down. Water was already beginning to puddle around her feet. "Nothing *to* do but evacuate. Get your survival kit on and let's deploy that life raft! Quickly!"

"*Hoi hoi!*"

The girls slid out of their harnesses, opened the lockers at their feet, pulled out survival kits, and slung them around their waists. Matsuri twisted around in her seat and pulled out the life raft from its storage compartment.

Yukari's hand went to a panel on the wall. She opened it,

revealing a single, large red button. She put her finger on it. "Get ready, I'm blowing the hatch!"

A dry report, like a pistol shot, went off over their heads, and the hatch flew upwards, away from the orbiter.

The two girls crawled out onto the hull and removed their helmets. A strong, mid-spring sun shone down on them. There was a light breeze.

"Where are we...?"

The capsule's dye marker had stained the water around it a fluorescent green, but the water only extended a few meters before it ended in a straight line of brick-colored tiles. Above the tiles stood a single sign that read: THE DRAGONFLIES THANK YOU FOR KEEPING OUR POND CLEAN! Beyond that were carefully cropped patches of lawn and neatly laid brick walkways. There was a greenhouse, a flower stand, and an aging nature observation post—the kind they put in school gardens for the science class to test water samples and the like.

Beyond that, she saw a concrete building, three stories high. Another building next to it was connected to the first by a covered walkway. Yukari turned around and saw more buildings on the other side. They were in a central courtyard surrounded by identical concrete buildings.

"I think we're okay, Yukari. Look at all those people!"

Yukari scanned the buildings. Faces filled every window. They were all wearing the same clothes. They were all girls.

"I know where we are," Yukari said. "I know where we are!"

"*Hoi?* Where's that?"

"Nellis!"

"Who?"

"We're at Nellis Girls Academy! We landed on my school!"

[ACT 4]

IT WAS RIGHT in the middle of second period classes at Nellis Academy when it happened. There was the sound of an explosion from the central courtyard, and rolls of red-and-white fabric came billowing past the windows. The girls ran to the windows to see something like a giant bottle of brandy floating in the pond, steam rising from its surface.

Moments later, a section of that surface popped open, and two figures wearing full-face helmets emerged.

One of them removed her helmet. When her long black hair spilled out, someone shouted, "Yukari! It's Yukari!"

Immediately there was another explosion—this time of voices—as the students cheered, drowning out the protests of their teachers. Students began boiling out of the classrooms into the hallways and streaming out into the courtyard around the pond. Over a thousand eyes were fixed on Yukari and Matsuri.

"Yukari, Yukari, it's me!"

"Matsuri!"

"Can I have your autograph?"

"Yukari, remember me? It's me, Eiko!"

"All students return to your classrooms immediately!"

"Yukari! Can I shake your hand?"

"Cool suits!"

"Miss Morita, remove your *spaceship* at once!"

"Quiet, Teach! This is a historical event!"

"Hey! She looked at me!"

"All students return to your classrooms immediately!"

"We've been rooting for you this whole time, Yukari!"

"Matsuri! Look over here! Let me take your picture!"

"Say something!"

"Somebody tell that principal to shut up!"

"Too bad you didn't hit *him* with your spaceship!"

"This is your principal speaking! All students return to your classrooms immediately! Anyone not back in their classroom will receive detention!"

No one left the courtyard.

Yukari stood frozen, her face stretched in an awkward grin.

"*Hoi?* They all look like you, Yukari," Matsuri whispered.

Yukari scanned the crowd of faces, all with hair cut to the same length, all wearing the same uniform. "I was right there in that crowd not too long ago."

Nellis Academy was famously strict, but when the floodgates opened, they opened for good. The courtyard was mass chaos. It was a mutiny, and Yukari had caused it. One of the teachers stepped forward and caught her eye.

Yukari remembered her. *Sachiko Yamashina, the Dragon Lady.* She taught classics.

"What is the meaning of this, Miss Morita? Class is in session!"

Wow, nothing fazes this woman. Can't she see that something's wrong—

"Ack!" Yukari bit her tongue. She'd forgotten about the goldfish. The power in the orbiter was off, which meant the goldfish didn't have long to live.

"Everyone, I need your help!" Yukari shouted, ignoring her teacher for the moment. The crowd fell silent. "Some goldfish we were using in an experiment are about to die. Anyone know anything about fish?"

"Goldfish?" The girls looked at one another.

Someone in the crowd said, "What about Akane? She'd know what to do!"

"Akane Miura? In 2-A?"

"Yeah, the one with the perfect grades."

"I'll go get her!"

Akane Miura... The name rang a bell. Yukari vaguely remembered her being at the top of the list when they posted test results from the first semester. A few moments later, part of the crowd began to whirl with excitement and a short, slender girl emerged, several hands pushing her forward.

Her hair was cut short, with fine bangs hanging down over her forehead. She wasn't wearing glasses. *Less the typical bookworm type and more the aspiring author type,* thought Yukari. The crowd pushed Akane right up to the edge of the pond. Despite the startled look on her face, her keen eyes shone as she took in the situation. Eventually, they rested on Yukari, standing on top of the orbiter.

"What's this about goldfish?" she asked in a soft voice.

Yukari held up the fish tank. "They're in here."

Akane leaned forward to get a better look.

Yukari hopped into the pond, and a ripple of excitement ran through the students. Waist deep in water, she waded up to the bank and crawled up onto land, handing the tank to Akane. "We were in orbit when their alarm went off."

The fish were dimly visible through the thick glass. Akane's face went pale.

"Oh no, we have to aerate their water right away! Let's bring them to the biology classroom. Come on!"

Akane led Yukari through the crowd, which quickly parted to let them through. Looking back toward the pond as she ran, Yukari shouted, "Stay there, Matsuri! Don't let anyone touch the orbiter!"

"Okay!"

"Everyone back to your rooms, NOW!"

The biology classroom was quiet. No classes were held there in the morning. Akane ran into the adjoining lab. Pulling an empty aquarium tank off the shelf, she filled it with water and added a packet of powder.

"You can just put them in here."

"Okay," Yukari said, then stopped. "Wait. The experiment requirements stipulated that we can't change the water."

"Oh." Akane frowned. "This connector thing here is what you use to cycle the water in their tank, right?"

"That's right. That's where the trouble happened. I think the QD might be jammed."

"The QD?"

"The quick disconnect. It's so you can pull off the tube without spilling any water."

Akane examined the port. "Well, can I put some air in, at least?"

"That should be all right."

"Then I think we might be able to save them."

"Really?"

Akane pulled a toolbox and some equipment in a cardboard box off another shelf. "Since the QD isn't working, I'm just going to take off the cover here and extract the water with this water pump. Then I can use this chamber to aerate the water and cycle it back in. We'll have to put a filter in between the two, though. How does that sound?"

"I'm not sure I follow, but it sounds great. Let's give it a try!"

"Will do."

Akane moved quickly. First she cut a length of silicon tubing, connecting one half to a small device and sticking the other inside the fish tank. Then she attached a bottle of oxygen to a regulator. Where the seals didn't quite fit, she used tape to close up the gaps. She flipped the switch on the bottle, and the water began to circulate.

"Hey, you did it!"

"We're not out of the woods yet." Akane took a small sample of water out of the fish tank with a pipette and dripped it onto a strip of test paper.

"I thought so. The ammonia concentration's way too high."

"Okay...so what do we do?"

"We could use other chemicals to neutralize it, but maybe that would violate your conditions?"

"Hmm, I wonder."

"Actually," Akane said, "now that I think about it, your testing equipment back on the ship must've used a similar method to extract the ammonia. Otherwise you'd have trouble keeping them alive."

"Okay, then. Let's do it."

"Right."

Akane quickly calculated the volume of water from the tank size, measured out an appropriate amount of neutralizing agent, and added it to the water.

"Oh, one other thing," she said. "We have to keep their water the right temperature. You know what the temperature was on your ship?"

"Erm..." Yukari scratched her head.

"I'm pretty sure this variety prefers 23°C, but if they were trying to breed them, they might've made it warmer."

"I don't think there was any breeding going on. Yeah, 23°C sounds about right."

"Good." Akane briefly stopped the pump and inserted a small heater and thermostat inside the chamber. "It will take a little time to warm up, but thankfully it's pretty close to the right temperature this time of year already."

"So that's it?"

"I think so."

"Whew!" Yukari gave a long sigh of relief. The goldfish had visibly improved. She looked up and smiled. "Sorry, I'm Yukari Morita. Thank you."

"Oh, uh, I'm Akane Miura."

Yukari offered to shake hands and Akane blushed.

"I remember your name," Yukari said. "You got top grades first semester, right?"

"And you were in Class B first year, right?"

"I'm surprised you remember me."

"You were really good in track, even though you're small like me. And then you, uh—"

"Dropped out because I got a job."

"Oh, I didn't mean to say—"

Just then, the door to the lab opened and a teacher appeared. "Yukari Morita! Just who is responsible for that *rocket ship* out there?"

"It's not a rocket ship, actually. It's an orbiter. And I'm the captain."

"Then come to the principal's office right this minute, 'Captain'!"

"Okay..." Yukari said, dazed. She turned back to Akane. "Watch the goldfish for me?"

"No problem," Akane said, a look of concern on her face as she watched the other girl leave.

[ACT 5]

THICK CARPETING COVERED the floor of the principal's office. Rows of golden figurines and plaques—trophies from various sporting events—lined the walls. Some calligraphy in a frame read NEVER GIVE UP. A large, heavy double-winged desk made out of some dark mahogany-like wood dominated the middle of the room.

"Um, you wanted to see me?" Yukari announced herself as she stepped gingerly into the room, her muddy space suit boots leaving tracks behind her.

Across the desk from her sat a man in silver-rimmed glasses, sparse hair combed in neat lines across the dome of his head. Blue veins were clearly visible across his brow, and the tension in his face sent ripples through the air. He spoke.

"Come to pay a visit to your old school?"

"Well, er, actually—"

"Oh, we have some miscreants at our school who think they can drive up in their sports cars or motorbikes, but this is the first time we've had someone in a spaceship!"

"Um, I'd sure hope—"

"And in that attire! Miss Morita, have you no shame?"

Yukari sighed. It wasn't like she was wearing a skintight space suit on purpose.

"You think you're above the rules, is that it? Or is this just another part of your *vendetta* against me?"

"Excuse me? Vendetta? Sir, I—"

"Yes, *I* was the one who expelled you. But I only did what any educator in my position would have done! This school strictly forbids our students from holding part-time jobs, and you did so, and quite *publicly*, I might add. How was I to set an example for the other students if I didn't punish you? That's how I explained my position to the regional school board—a position they approved, I'll have you know."

It was true, to a point. When she had first joined the Solomon Space Association program, they'd taken her on as a part-time employee. She had gone through the proper channels and applied for a semester off with the intention of returning in the third quarter—except that her unexpected expulsion hit before the paperwork was approved.

Now, if she had been expelled because she wasn't taking her classes seriously, she could understand that. But to be expelled for working a part-time job just because it was against the rules? That really ticked her off.

"Did you call me in here to make excuses?"

"What excuses?" the principal snorted. "Clearly I was right about your intentions today."

"I'm not here on some vendetta. Our landing in the school pond was a complete coincidence."

"You expect me to believe that out of all the places on Earth where you could have landed, your coming down on school property—your very own school's property—was a coincidence? Ridiculous!"

"I was as surprised as you are, sir, but the fact is that you just can't set an orbiter capsule down wherever you want to. Especially not when there are complications."

"Doesn't the space shuttle over in America land on its own runway every time? That's pretty pinpoint."

"That's because the space shuttle has flight controls. On our ship, once you open the parachute, you're at the mercy of the wind currents—"

"Nice try, but you won't pull the wool over *this* educator's eyes!"

"Well, I'm sorry, but you have no idea what you're talking about." Yukari stamped her foot. "And what's the big idea expelling me just because I broke one little rule!"

"Rules are rules, Miss Morita. And it is of the utmost importance to us that all of our girls learn the rules by which they must lead their lives before we send them out into society—"

"But I didn't *want* to leave. I wanted to come back!" There was an edge to Yukari's voice. "I was going to come back here after my first flight. I was going to ace my classes, pass my tests, get into a topflight university, and land a glamorous job at some company somewhere. I was going to have a normal life!" She was practically raging now.

A look of fear flashed across the principal's face. "Oh, you're on a vendetta, all right. You resent me."

"Of course I resent you! You're ruining my life on a—on a technicality!"

The principal waggled his finger at her. "I know what you're up to, Morita. You're going to use this newfound fame of yours to turn the media against me, aren't you. You're trying to get me fired from my job!"

Yukari blinked. "Huh? Of course I'm not."

"But you could if you tried. That's why you landed here, isn't it? This is a thinly veiled threat. You were trying to teach me a lesson."

Yukari rolled her eyes. "The only lesson I want you to learn here is that you Can't. Control. Where. An Orbiter. Splashes. Down!"

Yukari was in mid-rant when she heard a tremendous roar, the kind of sound you can feel in the pit of your stomach. The windows rattled and the room shook. She looked out to see an SDF navy helicopter hovering right outside the window.

"What, now the navy's here? What's all that racket?"

The helicopter was a Sikorsky MH-53E, the largest helicopter operating in Japanese airspace, with three 4400 hp gas turbine engines and a main rotor twenty-four meters in diameter. The local police, coast guard, and fire department wouldn't have a chopper that size. They must have called into the base for it when they heard what was coming down.

The windows of the building across the courtyard filled with faces. Behind her, the principal was screeching. "You called the SDF in, didn't you? Is there no end to your ambition, child?"

"I had nothing to do with it, really."

"Well you better get them out of here before the media descend upon us. I won't have you disrupting my classes any more than you already have!"

"Will you just shut up and let me deal with this?" Yukari pulled the transceiver from its pouch at her waist and thumbed the talk button. "This is the SSA spaceship *Rambutan*, hailing the navy helicopter currently over Nellis Academy. Come in, please."

"*Rambutan*, this is Big Bird with the SDF navy minesweeping division. We're here at the request of the Solomon Space Association, over."

"Thanks for coming."

"Not a problem. We'd like to get the retrieval started. Should we lower our men?"

"That's all right, we can handle it. I need you to take my copilot up in your sling now and myself after I get the orbiter hooked up."

"Roger that."

"It'll take me about ten minutes to get everything ready. Can you hold position for that long?"

"We'll manage."

"Where are you taking us, incidentally?"

"Our orders are to take you to the Space Lab in Sagamihara."

It looked like they'd be reporting in to the experiment lead sooner than she thought. "Roger that."

Yukari dashed out of the room, leaving the principal to work on his embolism alone.

Back in the biology lab, Akane had her face pressed to the fish container. She was tapping on the glass with one finger.

When she saw Yukari come in, the other girl smiled. "Your goldfish are doing great—"

"Akane! Thanks for rigging that up, but now we have to get it to the space laboratory by helicopter. Think you can modify it to run on battery power?"

"Uh, I don't see why not..."

"Right now?"

"O-okay!"

Akane searched the shelves, pulling out some dry cell batteries and a battery case, which she used to switch her contraption over to DC power.

"What should I put it in? A cardboard box, maybe?"

"Anything—whatever works."

Akane carefully placed the fish tank and assorted apparatuses inside a large cardboard box she found on another of the shelves, fixing everything in place with several strips of packaging tape. "I think that should do it."

"Er...really?" Yukari took a dubious look inside the box.

"I hope so," Akane replied, though she didn't sound very sure of herself.

A troubling thought occurred to Yukari. *What happens if it breaks midflight? Would I be able to fix it myself?*

The flight would be short enough, but any little mishap and the whole experiment could be a wash. She looked up at the other girl. "Think you could come with me?"

"What?" Akane's eyes went wide.

"I want you to ride in the helicopter and help me take care of the goldfish. Just in case."

"Well, I—"

"Pretty please?"

"I mean, I do want the goldfish to be safe, but—" Akane lowered her eyes. "I have classes..."

"Oh, who gives a crap about this crappy school and its crappy classes!" Yukari barked, surprised at her own anger.

Wow, I really am *a delinquent.*

She softened her voice. "Well, look, I'm sure classes are very important, but you don't understand. These goldfish—the scientist working on these spent fifteen years getting ready for this one single experiment."

"What? Fifteen whole years?"

"Yeah. Space experiments are usually so short you wouldn't think it, but apparently, the getting-ready part takes forever. That's why I really need to see this through, and we're so close. It'd blow hard if something happened now after all those poor fish have been through."

"No kidding..."

Akane gripped her fists so tightly, her knuckles turned white. A moment passed, then her face shot up. "I'll go!"

"That's the spirit!"

A gale force wind blew through the courtyard of the school.

Matsuri was busily bundling up the parachute and shutting it inside the orbiter's nose. Yukari stood at the edge of the pond, looking up at the helicopter and barking into her transceiver.

"We'll be picking up one extra person. Take up the girl behind me first. She's a civvy, so be gentle."

"Roger that. Lowering the harness now."

The helicopter descended until it was hovering just above the school buildings. A sliding door opened and something like a thick belt began to play out from one side. The helicopter pitched slightly forward to get one end of the belt into the pond in order to disperse any static electricity. Sand whipped up from the ground, stinging Yukari's cheek.

She grabbed hold of the harness with one hand and beckoned Akane over. The girl stepped up beside her, cardboard box under one arm and her other hand holding down her skirt.

Yukari passed the harness beneath Akane's armpits and attached the v-ring to the hook at the base. Then she took the cardboard box out from beneath the other girl's arm and gave it to her to hold with both hands.

"All you have to do is hang there. The people on the helicopter will do the rest. Got it?"

Akane nodded, a nervous look on her face.

Yukari gave the pilot a thumbs-up and Akane began to rise until she was close enough to the helicopter for one of the soldiers to grab her arm and pull her inside. Next, they plucked Matsuri off the top of the hatch. Meanwhile, Yukari waded through the tiny whitecaps rippling across the pond to scramble up one side of the orbiter.

"Okay," Yukari said through her transceiver, "next up is the orbiter. It's taken on some water, so it should be a good four to five tons!"

"No problem. Lowering the freight hook."

"I'm ready for you."

A large hook used for carrying minesweeping equipment extended from directly beneath the main rotor.

"Just one meter more, that's it. Come forward, keep it slow."

The helicopter pilot made some minute adjustments, expertly compensating for the inertia of the hook. Yukari braced herself against the wind and shouted into her transceiver.

"Steady, steady, steady—all right."

Grabbing the heavy hook with both hands, she passed the hook through the carabiner on the parachute harness.

"She's all hooked up. My turn!"

Yukari jumped back into the pond and grabbed the harness that came swinging down. She pulled it around behind her back, attached the hook, and gave the thumbs-up. Matsuri and Akane were already buckled into seats along one wall when Yukari arrived. Akane sat rigid, cradling the cardboard box in her arms like a child holds a stuffed animal.

"You okay, Akane? We're safe now."

"Y-yeah."

The pilot turned and shouted back to Yukari. "Okay to take her up?"

"Go for it! The water will spill out, so take it slow."

"Roger."

The pilot's bronzed left hand tensed and the whine of the turbine engine grew noticeably louder.

Yukari peeked out from the helicopter to take a look at the scene below. The seven blades of the main rotor had created a dust storm in the courtyard the likes of which Yukari had never seen. It looked like the gardening club's greenhouse had collapsed. Every tulip in the planters lay flat, and one or two of the older planters had completely disintegrated. *Oops.*

The cable connecting them to the orbiter went taut and the orbiter began to move, sloshing water from inside.

"Your craft's at a bit of an angle," the soldier manning the winch shouted. "That okay?"

"No problem. That's how it's supposed to lift!"

The soldier shouted something into an intercom, giving directions to the pilot.

The helicopter slowly began to rise.

The wind from the rotor blades turned the water spilling from the orbiter into a fine white mist spraying every which way across the courtyard. Every window in the school buildings and even the rooftops were filled with students waving and cheering.

Yukari waved back.

Goodbye, Nellis Academy. She didn't imagine she would ever be coming back there.

One of the soldiers closed the sliding door. At last, it was quiet enough inside the helicopter to talk normally. Once they leveled out, Yukari went up to the cockpit and greeted the pilot. "That went really well. I'm Yukari Morita, captain of the orbiter you're carrying."

"Commander Kimura with the Fifteenth Minesweeper Company," the middle-aged pilot announced brightly, turning his tanned face to look back at his passenger. "I have to admit I was surprised. I've seen your ship on television a number of times, but I never expected it to come down here."

"We were just as surprised as you. I didn't expect the SDF to come pick us up, either."

"The Coast Guard sent us. They've never retrieved an orbiter, and they wanted to make sure they had enough horsepower to do the job—speaking of which, Petty Officer Kuwabara!"

"Sir!" One of the soldiers answered from the back.

"Get up here and take a picture of us!"

"Yes, sir!"

"Here, I'll turn around and look back so he can get both our faces."

"Huh?"

Petty Officer Kuwabara motioned to the other two girls. "Why don't you get in too?"

"*Hoi!* I love pictures! Let's go, Akane!"

"What? Me?"

"Yeah. Don't you want to remember the moment?"

Grinning like a madwoman, Matsuri undid Akane's harness. Akane gently set down her cardboard box and came up to the front.

"Commander, I'd like to get in the shot as well, if I could," another of the soldiers called out. "Me too!" said another.

"Maybe I could get one with just Yukari first—"

"I want one with Matsuri!"

"I'll take one with the girl in the Nellis uniform."

They took pictures in various combinations as the helicopter swiftly made its way toward Sagamihara airspace. They were almost at their destination when the helicopter from the Kanagawa Police Department caught up to them.

"Someone told the Space Lab we were coming, right?" Yukari asked.

"Affirmative," the pilot told her.

Yukari peered out the front window. "That straight line right there is the Yokohama Train Line, which means...is that it?"

"That's the place."

Several perfectly square buildings formed a small compound below. There was a green in the very middle and a thin rocket on a display stage off to one side.

The helicopter hovered over the green until someone from the lab came running out to direct them. Slowly, the copter began to descend, the orbiter drawing closer to its own shadow cast on the grass until the two met. The orbiter toppled on its side and the helicopter gently set down a short distance away. The sliding door flew open, and the crew jumped out to secure the landing zone.

"Time to go." Yukari motioned to Akane.

Shrinking away from the idling rotor above her head, Akane left the chopper, led by the two astronauts. One of the helicopter crew was busily unhooking the orbiter.

A man in his mid-fifties wearing a suit and necktie came running from the main building.

It's Miyamoto, thought Yukari. Professor Miyamoto was head researcher in charge of the goldfish experiment—or more accurately, the vestibular adaptation experiment. She remembered him from his visits a month before to the Solomon base for a practice run. He had been running around then too. He was a likable man, with short legs, a chubby belly, and bushy eyebrows.

Miyamoto wiped the sweat from his forehead with a handkerchief and greeted them. "Hello there! Welcome, welcome! I'd arrgh—" The professor's voice was lost in the sound of the helicopter taking off.

Yukari turned and saluted the crew. In a matter of moments, the helicopter receded into the distance and relative silence returned to the complex. Yukari turned back around to face the professor.

"Well, we're back. We landed in Yokohama, of all places."

"So I heard, so I heard. I certainly wasn't expecting you to get here so soon, that's for certain. Well, how are they? Still living?"

"They're right here."

Yukari pointed at the cardboard box in Akane's hands.

Akane offered up her box, and Professor Miyamoto thrust his face inside. He was a bit nearsighted.

"Hey! They *are* still alive! Doing quite well, as a matter of fact! All right!" His head popped back out. "Well, this is really something! Thank you! Thank you so much!" One by one, he grabbed each of their hands in turn and gave them a vigorous shake. Yukari half expected him to shed a joyful tear or two. She smiled.

"Akane threw that transport container together all by herself!"

"You don't say? Very nice, very, very nice!" Hefting the box in his left arm, Miyamoto gripped Akane's hand and pumped it vigorously.

"Sorry—I know it doesn't look like much."

"Not at all, not at all. Now, quickly, to the lab!" The professor scurried off, muttering happily to himself as he left.

Akane shook her head, watching him leave.

"He seems happy," Yukari said. "If I didn't know any better, I'd say he was going to start skipping any moment now."

"No kidding," Akane said, allowing herself a little chuckle.

Far ahead of them already, the professor turned and shouted, "What are you waiting for? Come on, come on. You have to tell me about everything!"

[ACT 6]

EVERY SCREEN IN the control room was off. The only thing moving was the countdown clock in one corner. T PLUS I DAY 2 HR 17 MIN 5 SEC. At the rearmost terminal in the central row, chief controller Kazuya Kinoshita was on the phone.

"I see... So the goldfish were okay? ...Right. Good job. ...No, OECF Operations should take care of that. What about today? Sure, just keep it under control. Right. Take it easy."

Quietly, he set down the receiver and raised his voice. "Everyone, listen up. Our astronauts are at the Space Lab. This wraps up control operations for this mission. It may not have been pretty, but we did it. Good job, everyone."

There was no clapping. Everyone seated at the terminals stood up as one, stretched, and began collecting their papers.

Kinoshita jotted something down in his logbook and went into the guest room to report to Nasuda. "The orbiter and its crew have arrived at the Space Lab. The craft took a little damage, but the goldfish are fine. Our astronauts are giving their report to Professor Miyamoto now. The girls plan on staying at Yukari's house tonight."

"I see. Well then, the mission was a success."

"A partial success, maybe."

"Success is success. All's well that ends well, right?"

Nasuda turned to Director Holden and spoke in English. "As you can see, our mission was a complete success. We accomplished a second test flight with a multiple-seat orbiter, broadcast video of a spacewalk, and completed our vestibular adaptation experiment using goldfish."

"A complete success?" The director raised an eyebrow. "I seem to recall a malfunction in your test equipment, aberrant departure from orbit, lost position, and emergency splashdown. These matters don't concern you at all?"

"I admit there were some events that we failed to predict," Nasuda said, "yet our crew and test subjects have returned unharmed. Their actions in orbit and our response on the ground kept it together."

"To me it seems like there was a fair bit of luck involved," the director said with a shake of his head. "Thank you for inviting me here. It was certainly a fascinating experience, I'll give you that. The SSA's work is worthy of attention. After all, this is the third manned space program after the U.S. and Russia, and you've shown impressive results while managing to maintain a far-smaller-scale operation."

"That we have." Nasuda was practically beaming.

"But let me be frank. I'm afraid that, all things considered, it would be premature for your program to participate in the construction of an international space station."

"But, Director—"

Holden raised a hand, cutting off Nasuda mid-objection. "Don't get me wrong. We're not trying to hold you back or make you toe the line. Our shuttle fleet is overworked. We need all the help we can get. And we know you are the only ones with the skintight space suit technology and hybrid engines." Holden stood. "But your results are still weak. I look forward to more progress from you in the future."

[ACT 7]

MIYAMOTO'S LABORATORY ROOM was utter chaos.

Desks, computers, bookshelves, and storage racks were packed along the walls, surrounding a single workstation desk the size of an automobile in the very center of the room. Other than the narrow corridor on all sides of the workstation, every flat surface in the room was covered with piles of stuff.

Professor Miyamoto cleared a space on top of the desk and set down the cardboard box. Mumbling to himself, he removed the fish container. A similar device was already sitting on top of the workstation with all of its wiring and tubing exposed—a prototype, Yukari assumed.

"It does look like the QD is plugged with...poop? Yes, that's poop all right."

He took off the lid and began to clean the area around the QD with a paintbrush and a syringe. When he had finished, he placed the container in the prototype device and flicked on the switch. The water began to circulate.

"There, that should do it. Too bad you can't do that up in space."

"You'd get water all over the place."

"No doubt. Sorry it had to break down right before reentry."

"Actually, it was more like during our reentry. It was a little hard to do the experiment and pilot at the same time," Yukari said.

"If the orbiter was a little larger, that might be possible."

"I hear they're working on an orbiter that seats three," Matsuri said.

"You don't say?" The professor pulled up some chairs to his own desk and sat the girls down. He was examining the cardboard box they had brought.

"You did a fine job with this. Something of a genius at make-shift repairs, are you?"

"No, nothing like that," Akane stammered, blushing.

"It took us fifteen years to get this device to its current level," the professor said. "No one had ever built an aquarium for space before. I went around asking everyone for help. That oxygen regulator came from an artificial lung the medical department was working on."

Akane nodded, eyes wide.

"The filter was a tough nut to crack too. We had to consider all the possibilities, like what would happen if they laid eggs on top of it, and what kind of material to use, and whether or not to use zeolite to get rid of the ammonia. We tested everything.

"But if someone told me to repair this thing on the spot, I'm not sure what I would have done. You have some experience with animals in a laboratory setting?"

"I'm in charge of the aquarium and the terrarium in our biology class. Though I don't really do much—just take care of them and make observations."

"That's plenty! I'm sure you come away with quite a lot from that."

"I do," Akane said, visibly pleased. "Actually, I was wondering if I could ask you something."

"Anything."

"What exactly were you testing with these goldfish?"

"Whether or not vestibular adaptability can be learned," the professor said, his voice rising. He was clearly happy she had asked. "We wanted to see how quickly goldfish that had already been in space would relearn on their second flight. If there was an observable learning effect, then we might be able to find out exactly *where* the goldfish are keeping that information—that was our goal."

"Fascinating!"

"Vestibular functions are thought to be related to space sickness.

And space sickness gets in the way of spaceflight, as you know."

"Sure. It's like seasickness that lasts for the first few days of a flight, right?" Akane asked.

"That's correct. Of course, there are a lot of other challenges out there waiting for an astronaut. Things like calcium deficiencies due to radiation and the redistribution of body fluids. But humanity must move into space sooner or later. You agree?"

"Of course."

"We're constantly fighting about this religion or that ideology or some territory or another down here. Well, my thinking is: why not just move away from all that? If the earth gets too cramped, we can settle space. It starts with the station. Next the moon. Then Mars. Some scientists have even proposed moving to comets. Imagine that, comets! That's why we have to overcome all of the hurdles between us and these, er, 'lofty' goals. This experiment is one small part of that, a fragment of the answer, if you will. You agree?"

"Of course!"

"If one experiment fails, we can't move on to the next. That's why I needed you to bring those goldfish back alive. Here I thought all was lost, but then *you* came to the rescue." Miyamoto beamed and clapped Akane on the shoulder. "It's that kind of quick thinking that makes you an astronaut, I guess! Splendid, splendid!"

Akane blinked. "Er, actually, sir, I'm not—"

"She's a civilian," Yukari cut in. "She just happened to be there at the school where we landed."

"What? Is that so? Why, I was sure the SSA had sent you!"

"No, actually. See, we landed at Nellis Academy—"

Yukari went on to tell the entire story of their emergency splashdown and subsequent efforts to keep the goldfish alive. Miyamoto listened attentively, scratching his head throughout.

"I see, I see! Well, I suppose I can be forgiven the misunderstanding. After all, she's the right age, and the girl does have considerable talent."

Apparently, he hadn't noticed that Akane was wearing her school uniform.

The professor chuckled. "I swear, I can't look at a short schoolgirl these days without wondering if she's an astronaut."

"A short schoolgirl..." Yukari glanced over at Akane. The girl was roughly the same height as she was, maybe even a little slighter in build. Perfect height, perfect weight. She wished someone like Akane had been there when everything started going haywire. Someone to watch the experiments while she and Matsuri focused on piloting. That would have made everything so much easier. Matsuri was clearly giving Akane the once-over as well.

Well, it can't hurt to ask.

"Say, Akane. Want a job?"

"What kind of job?"

"Oh, I don't know. Like, maybe being an astronaut for the SSA?"

Akane burst out laughing. "You're pulling my leg!"

"Nope. No leg-pulling."

"*Hoi!* What a great idea." Matsuri joined in. "Boy, with Akane on the team, we'd be golden!"

"We haven't made any public announcements, but truth be told, we really need someone. This could be your big chance, Akane. Really."

"But, but I couldn't be an astronaut. Don't you have to be in great physical condition?"

"A little training would take care of that, no problem."

"But..."

"Boy, if it was me, I'd be there in a heartbeat," Miyamoto said. "Surely you must have your share of applicants? You're quite popular these days."

"Actually, we do," Yukari said. While it was true that they had made no public announcement, every month, one or two hopefuls made their way to the Solomon Space Center—on a tiny island at the edge of civilization, a place devoid of any entertainment or anything to do at all if one wasn't in the SSA already. Most people who wanted to be the next Yukari or Matsuri despaired the moment they set foot in the place.

There were a few whose passion to go into space overcame any such concerns, but every one of them had been physically unsuited for the job. Even though they never put it into words, the SSA wasn't in the position to even consider anyone who wasn't under 155 centimeters tall and weighed less than thirty-eight kilograms. Also, though it wasn't an absolute requirement, they really preferred a girl. The lack of a toilet onboard the orbiter would make things complicated were males integrated into the crew.

Which was why the best people gave up on the SSA and instead went for the Space Development Agency back in Japan. A successful career there could get you on the space shuttle and even get you a chance for a stay on the ISS.

There were other reasons holding some applicants back. Even though the space shuttle wasn't really all that safe, and the SSA wasn't as dangerous as it seemed, people thought twice about actually stepping into Yukari's shoes when it came down to it. Not even the lure of overnight fame was sufficient temptation.

"I should think all you'd need is your health. I mean, if the shoe fits wear it, right? And I think you'd fit just right, Akane."

Akane frowned, unconvinced.

Miyamoto stared at her. "You seem more the research type than a member of a flight crew. You like biology?"

"Yes," she replied. Then, more enthusiastically, "Ever since I was in elementary school!" Now Akane began to talk faster than Yukari had ever heard her talk. "We had to observe morning glories for a summer project in third grade, and I got to wondering why it was that some of them had vines that twisted to the right and others had vines twisting to the left. I couldn't figure it out just by looking at the ones we had on our patio, so I ended up examining every morning glory on my block, then I went to the next block and the next until I had examined one hundred plants in all. When I averaged them out, right-twisting vines came out to fifty-three percent."

Miyamoto laughed out loud. "So no statistically significant difference, then."

"Well, I didn't know about statistical analysis back then, so my conclusion was that right-twisting morning glories were more common. My teacher was really impressed, and I guess I let it go to my head. Oh, that's right, I even did a sort of fake space experiment when I was in junior high."

"You don't say?"

"I couldn't pull off a zero-gravity experiment, but I could make a high-G experiment right here on Earth. I modified an old record player into a centrifuge. Then I put a tulip bulb in some dirt at the edge and spun it around at 2 G to see what would happen."

"Very interesting!" Miyamoto exclaimed. "They've raised chickens using that same method in America, and the Germans similarly observed jellyfish in space, you know. It must've taken quite some time for you to get any results."

"Well, that's the thing. I put the centrifuge out on the patio and let it spin all night and day. My mom wanted me to stop—she was afraid the record player was going to burst into flames or something—so I promised her I would keep my eye on it, and I ended up sitting there for three whole days. In the end, on the eighth day, the record player broke, so I never *did* get any results. But my science teacher was still impressed and told me that if I really wanted to become a scientist when I grew up, I would also need to study math and English and take tests so I could get into good schools. I think that's around when I started to really like studying."

"You mean you can grow into liking studying?" Yukari asked.

"I always thought it was something you were born either liking or hating."

"No, I really think you can learn to like it. It's like getting this new tool to think with, and the more you study, the more you understand—like how you can use a single guideline to solve geometry problems, or how great it feels to figure out a proof, or the fun in using simple English vocabulary to say complicated things, or the fun in reading the newspaper after you learn about something in social studies, and because every class has tests, you get immediate results—it's so satisfying! And then —" Akane shook her head. "What am I saying? I'm sorry. I get carried away sometimes." She blushed and covered her face with her hands.

"Not at all, not at all." Miyamoto smiled. "It was a fascinating story. Why, it's people like you that give me hope for the future of the sciences in this country. Have you already picked a university?"

"I want to go to Tokyo University and study molecular biology under Professor Niuchi."

"Ah yes, Dr. Niuchi. That's a good school. And molecular biology is fascinating."

Akane's face shone. "I mean, I know life is sacred, but you can't just call it sacred and leave it at that. You have to get to the bottom of things to really understand them, and I figured that molecular biology would be the place to start."

"Quite right. I began with physics myself, but your approach is sound."

"You really think so?"

"So this is what it's like to be a star student," Yukari said with disbelief. "You know exactly what you're going to do after you graduate already?"

"Well, I'm already a junior!"

"Oh yeah, right..." Yukari scratched her head. Yukari had never made it to her junior year. Still, she wondered if she would have been quite so certain about her own future as Akane seemed to be.

"Still," Yukari said, trying to steer the conversation back, "they have adult tests you can take for credits, and you can always study. You don't have to be in school to do that. It wasn't me who first said this, but if you really want to study something, space is the place."

"Yes," Akane said, a faraway look in her eyes, "I suppose you're right."

There's that look, thought Yukari—the look someone got when they first pictured themselves actually being in space. Yukari had seen it a number of times since starting her current job. She had already been on four orbital flights. She was used to zero gravity, the stress of takeoff and reentry, and dealing with the media. But the one thing she was sure she would never grow tired of was the view from space.

It was impossible to put into words or images. They always asked her about it in interviews, and all she could say was her set response: if you really want to know, you have to come see for yourself.

How would she answer Akane if she asked? She didn't want to give her usual cookie-cutter response, and yet...

"I guess it's the kind of thing that you can't know without going to see for yourself," Akane said suddenly.

Yukari gaped, her eyes going to the other girl's face. Akane's eyes were clear as water, staring straight at her.

That was a funny coincidence.

"You want to come with me?" Yukari found herself saying.

Akane said nothing for a moment. Then her eyes drifted downward. "No. No, I think I'm more the study-at-my-desk type."

"Oh..." Yukari gave a little sigh. *Maybe I was getting ahead of myself.*

"I'm sorry, I didn't mean to pressure you or anything."

"No, not at all."

When she thought about it, it had been a crazy thing to ask. *Hey, you, want to become an astronaut?* Still, Akane looked a little sad now that Yukari had effectively rescinded the offer.

"Hey," Yukari said, "if you change your mind, give me a call, will you? You can just phone the Solomon Islands and ask the operator to connect you to the SSA."

"Okay."

"Right, time for the debriefing. Tell me everything that happened after liftoff," Miyamoto said.

"Right." Yukari shook her head. "Well—"

Immediately following a spaceflight, astronauts were subjected to a slew of questions. The goal was to get all the details of everything that had happened while their memories were still fresh, so that what they learned could benefit future missions. This was called debriefing.

Yukari glanced at her notes. "So around 0130, they started looping a lot and rolling."

"They were swimming all over the place," Matsuri added.

"Yeah, it was almost hard to watch them. They looked really tired."

The professor found the time stamp on the telemetry graph. "It looks like they were panicking because of a drop in the concentration of diffused oxygen. The goldfish were too active. Did you notice anything different inside the aquarium?"

"I saw one or two scales sparkling at the bottom," Matsuri said.

"Those were scales?" Yukari asked. "You have better eyes for the natural world than I do, Matsuri."

"Um..." Akane said. "I should probably get going."

Yukari had completely forgotten. "Oops! That's right. We kind of took her out of school in the middle of classes."

"Oh, is that so? Sorry to keep you so long," the professor said.

"No, it's been great, really. I'd love to be able to stay longer if I could—but if I leave now I might make it in time for afternoon classes."

"Well, you're welcome back anytime. I've got plenty of things I'd love to show you here."

"Thank you so much!"

The professor smiled and handed her his card. "I'll call a taxi for you. Don't worry, it's on us." He picked up the phone.

"No, I can walk."

"It's farther away than you think. Don't worry, we owe you at least this much."

While they were standing at the front gate waiting for the taxi to arrive, Yukari spoke with Akane. "Sorry about all this. I know Nellis is really hard on people skipping class."

"I think they'll understand," the other girl replied. "After all, it was for a good cause."

"Well, I hope so."

"And I had a really great time."

"Just think, if you were an astronaut, every day would be like this."

Akane chuckled nervously. Yukari joined her.

"Sorry, I didn't mean to be pushy."

"No, I really appreciate it. Thanks for inviting me."

The taxi arrived.

Yukari, Matsuri, and Miyamoto stood at the curb and waved goodbye.

[ACT 8]

IT WAS ALREADY evening when debriefing was over. After a simple press conference, the two astronauts left the Space Lab by taxi.

"Hey, are you those two astronauts? Yukari and Matsuri, was it?" the driver asked.

They both nodded.

"Neat! Those your space suits? Do you always wear those?"

"No. Today is kind of...special." Yukari explained what had happened. The driver's face in the rearview mirror looked surprised.

"Well, it must be tough flying around up there so fast!"

"Yeah, and it's too cramped to bring a change of clothes. That's where we're going now—to get new things to wear."

"Downtown, right?"

"Yeah. If you could head into the shopping district from one of the side streets. We kind of stick out in these."

"No problem. Leave it to me."

"Oh, I should ask, can we use American Express for this?"

"No problem."

The survival kit they were supplied with held a roll of U.S. ten-dollar bills and an American Express card. It wasn't perfect, but it worked well enough in emergencies. This, Yukari had already decided, was an emergency—and buying civilian clothes in the department store counted as survival in the broadest sense of the word.

The taxi was entering the streets of downtown Yokohama. Matsuri was glued to the window, staring at the unfamiliar sights outside.

"What a busy place!"

Matsuri was practically leaning out of the car as they waited for a light to change. Yukari dragged her back inside.

"C'mon, we stand out bad enough as it is."

"But they love us!"

Matsuri waved her hands vigorously at people on the street. A group of high school students stopped, their mouths hanging open.

"Will you knock that off?"

They were in the shopping district now.

"How's this?" the driver asked.

"One more block. There. Right behind that building."

They got out of the taxi, crossed over one wide street, and went straight into a boutique on the other side of the intersection. Yukari had been going there since she was in junior high. She used to stop by on her way to school.

"Hiya!"

"Hello...hey! Yukari! Long time no see! How are you?" The owner, a tall man with a touch of hair on his chin, came out. He checked the girls out from head to toe.

"I like the threads! Takes a little bit of courage to wear those in broad daylight, but I approve!"

"Well, I don't," Yukari said. "We basically came here straight from the Space Lab up in Sagamihara. You think you can find something for us to wear?"

"Can I ever! What are you in the mood for?"

"I was thinking maybe a simple dress with something on top— or is that not cool these days?"

"Honey, it's all in the coordination. Just you watch and see."

"Great, well, whatever works."

"Leave it to me! What about shoes? I think I might have some sandals in here somewhere."

"Great, thanks!"

The owner flitted about picking out items until Yukari was holding a miniskirt dress and a short-sleeved cardigan. For her feet, she had platinum white sandals.

"And your name is Matsuri, right? What sort of look are we aiming for here?"

"*Hoi!* I want something like that!" Matsuri said, pointing at the mannequin in the shop window.

"Showing a bit of skin in the middle, then? Perfect! That will look great on you."

While he was gathering Matsuri's outfit, Yukari went into the dressing room to change.

First, she had to take off the adapter ring around her neck.

Between the adapter ring and her neck was a thin rubber membrane, which served to keep the air in her helmet separate from the air inside her suit. A special adhesive was used between the membrane and the skin of her neck, which made taking it off a little like peeling back a Band-Aid—painful.

The space suit was one solid piece, and in order to remove it, she had to undo the airtight fasteners from her throat all the way down to her crotch. She peeled the suit off her arms and legs like a rubber glove, leaving the outfit inside out.

The suit was made out of a miracle fabric that was airtight, pressurized, and insulated, yet it also wicked away sweat, allowing the skin to maintain its own temperature.

In a sense, the skintight space suits were like a second skin, specially adapted for space. There was no room underneath them even for underwear. The owner of the shop was right. It did take a bit of courage to wear the suits outdoors.

Yukari finished changing and left the dressing room.

The owner took a look at the space suit hanging from her arm limply like a deflated doll. "Say, you don't think you could sell me one of those? I'd love to put it up in my shop window."

"Well, they're seventeen million yen a pop."

"Yikes! For real?"

"These are actual flight models, yep. Apparently, even *that* is pretty cheap as far as space suits go. But I'm afraid I can't sell it anyway—the design is top-secret. We're discouraged from even taking them off when we're not on base."

"I see, I see," the owner said, clearly giving up. "Well, do you think I could at least advertise that you came here? It's not every shop in Yokohama that gets visits from astronauts. I could put up a picture of you two."

"Sure, no problem," Yukari said, smiling. "I could even sign the picture for you if you like."

"Ooh, that'd be great! Thanks!"

A few moments later, Matsuri came out of the other dressing room. "*Hoi!* What do you think?"

Matsuri was wearing a bikini top with a sleeveless shirt over it and skimpy bikini bottoms under a pair of hip huggers.

"It's practically a swimsuit—though you look completely natural in that, I'll admit."

"A perfect fit, if you ask me," the owner beamed. "Now for the final touch." He picked out a pair of sunglasses and propped them up on Matsuri's head. "There! Splendid! Quick, let's take a photo!"

The owner brought out a camera, had the two girls stand in one corner of the shop, and started clicking away.

They paid with the emergency credit card, and shoving their space suits in the bottom of a shopping bag, emerged onto the busy streets.

"Hey!"

"*Hoi?*"

Yukari was staring at a sign for a beauty parlor across the street. Her head started itching. "Let's go in there."

"A beauty salon? What do they do there?"

"We can get our hair washed and even put on a little makeup."

"Sounds like fun!"

The two dashed into the store.

"Can I get a wash and a cut, just even the sides up. Oh, and a little foundation."

"Absolutely," the beautician crisply replied.

Now that's service, Yukari thought. There was a big difference between a beauty salon in the middle of Yokohama and the dingy shack that passed for a salon back on Maltide.

"What's that?" Matsuri asked, looking around the shop while a hairdresser tried desperately to keep her bangs straight.

"Oh, that's nail art," her hairdresser told her. "You stick those on your nails. The simpler ones are stickers. For something fancier we have imitation jewels."

"Ooh! Neat!"

Matsuri's tribe had a tradition of painting themselves for festivals with body paint made of rendered pig fat mixed with natural pigmentation, like the local red soil. Apparently, nail art scratched Matsuri's cultural itch in a very direct way.

"Makita, could you do her nails?" the stylist asked one of the girls standing off to the side. The store nail specialist walked over and showed Matsuri a catalog. She chose a crimson manicure with topaz rhinestones.

"You do it too, Yukari. It's so pretty!"

Yukari frowned. She didn't want to go overboard. "Maybe just a manicure." Then she added, "But since we're wearing sandals, we should do our toes too, don't you think?"

When they were done being fussed over from head to toe—literally—Yukari felt like a new woman. They hit the street and took in the downtown air, a potent mélange of Italian food, perfume, and exhaust.

Not bad. Not bad at all.

"Time to go shopping!"

For their first stop, Yukari went into a CD store. "Let's see, I wonder if ZIMA has a new song...hey! They've got a whole a new album out! Score! And didn't Satsuki say she liked Hiroshi Itsuki? Might make a good present for her—you want something, Matsuri?"

"Sure. Anything fun?"

"Hmm. I'm guessing you'd like samba...over on that rack there."

"Wow. There's so many different kinds." Matsuri grabbed two fistfuls of samba CDs, five in each hand.

Next was the bookstore. Yukari picked out five books from the world affairs section and a current slang and jargon dictionary—the kind that came with a CD-ROM.

"Maybe I should read Takashi Tachibana's book about space. He'll probably be dropping by for an interview one of these days.

Oh, right, manga! Hey! Volume 7 of *Aoi and Ryoichi* is out! Gotta get that one—"

She glanced over at Matsuri to see her picking out some magazines from a large rack.

"*World Fishing*? You going fishing, Matsuri?"

"No, I like this fish!" she replied, pointing at the king salmon on the cover. "Very handsome."

"Um, okay," Yukari said. When it came to Matsuri, there was such a thing as too much information. She'd only wear herself out trying to follow her half sister's thought processes.

For an early dinner, they went into an Italian restaurant. Yukari wolfed down a crispy pizza with a paper-thin crust and topped it off with a piece of tiramisu. It seemed like forever since she'd eaten proper food in a restaurant.

Matsuri had ordered a plate of spaghetti, drowned it in a sea of mayonnaise, ketchup, and tabasco sauce, then proceeded to cram it into her mouth. On the side she had a glass of tomato juice into which she had also poured tabasco sauce. When it came to food, Matsuri's taste was simple: red is good.

When she was full, Yukari said, "Well now. Seeing as it's seven o'clock, I think we should call an official end to our survival operations for the day."

"You know," Matsuri said between mouthfuls, "I could get used to this kind of survival."

"You said it!"

Piling their shopping bags and space suits into a taxi, they set off toward the quiet residential district of Nogeyama. It had been ten months since Yukari had seen her home. It looked exactly the same. The front yard was simple, just a close-cropped lawn without a garden. The house itself was a three-story affair her mother had built with her own savings from her work as an architectural designer.

Her mother was the only resident now, but no lights were on.

The front door was locked, and no one answered when Yukari pressed the doorbell intercom button.

"Maybe she's on a business trip?"

There was a keypad by the door. Yukari entered her security number and the door opened. By her mother's request, all the lighting and climate control in the house was connected to a single button in the vestibule. When Yukari pressed it, the house lit up and the air conditioning came on.

Pulling a bottle of ginger ale out of the refrigerator, Yukari threw herself down onto the sofa in the living room. "It's true what they say," she said, "there's no place like home."

She turned on the television. It was the news. They were showing an aerial shot of a very familiar-looking scene.

"*...It was just time for second period classes to begin at Nellis Academy when a spacecraft suddenly landed in the school's garden pond, causing quite a disturbance. Strangely enough, the school is none other than Yukari Morita's alma mater...*"

"Hey! We're on!" Yukari shouted.

The news switched to the principal, standing with the school courtyard behind him. "*Yes, well, uh, I was happy to let bygones be bygones and focus our efforts on making sure everyone was okay—*"

"What a doofus. He's sweating bullets."

The reporter was asking him about Akane now.

"*Yes, well, we're still looking into reports that a student at our school assisted the astronauts, so I, er, have no comment about that at this time.*"

Yukari lifted an eyebrow. "What? He should be crowing about it to the world! A lot of taxpayer money went into that experiment she saved."

"*Hoi...* He's using a lot of complicated words," Matsuri said.

"I don't think he has any idea what he's saying, Matsuri."

"*Er, concerning the disfiguring of our garden, we are going to be processing a damage report and cost analysis and will be bringing that to the Solomon Space Association in hopes that proper restitution will be made—"*

Yukari shook her head. "Can you believe this guy? I mean, I feel bad for the gardening club, but boy, if we had hit anywhere else..."

"True, true."

"Those Taliho curses get more frightening all the time."

Yukari wasn't the only one who had started to lend more credence to the influence that the spirits of the Taliho tribe—the people living closest to the SSA base—had on their rockets and orbiters.

Yukari's missions had been plagued with difficulties. She wasn't the kind to believe in bad luck, but surely the number of sheer coincidences they'd had to face was reaching a probability of zero. They might be operating at the very cutting edge of science, but with all of the things going on, Yukari couldn't help but feel like their space program had less to do with science and more to do with the supernatural.

"I thought they made cursing our program illegal anyway. Are those villagers still doing their ceremonies?" Yukari asked.

"You're wrong," Matsuri said, shaking her head. "This wasn't a Taliho curse, Yukari. This was your curse."

"Huh?"

"You cursed that school of yours—maybe not out loud, but somewhere, deep inside your heart. You resented how they treated you. Your negative feelings summoned an evil spirit."

Yukari guffawed. "I don't mean to burst your bubble, Matsuri, but I'm not the curse-throwing type."

Matsuri looked over at her and calmly asked, "You know someone else who would want to curse that school?"

[ACT 9]

AKANE FOUND HERSELF being called into the principal's office. In all honesty, she hadn't seen it coming. She knew that technically, she had been truant. But she firmly believed that it had been for a good cause. She wouldn't have even been surprised if they had given her some kind of award.

But here she was enduring this, this *inquisition*.

"So," the school counselor said for the tenth time, "Yukari Morita coerced you into getting onto that helicopter. Isn't that right?"

"No, it isn't," Akane said once again. "She asked me if I would join them, and I went of my own free will."

How many times did they have to go through this? What do these people want to know?

"You sure you weren't coerced?"

"All Miss Morita said was that the experiment was really important. And when I met the researcher conducting the experiment, he confirmed that. They were investigating vestibular functions in goldfish as a way of determining optimal environments for people in space—"

"We're not concerned with any of that. So basically, you were threatened with the failure of this very important experiment and found yourself unable to refuse. Right?"

Not concerned? What?!

Akane grew increasingly sure that something wasn't right here.

"They were so grateful to me for saving those goldfish," Akane said, desperation creeping into her voice. "Why aren't you?"

CHAPTER TWO

OF FIGS AND SWALLOWS

[ACT 1]

IF YOU LOOK at a globe, just to the east of New Guinea and south of the red line of the equator lies a small chain of islands stretching from the northwest to the southeast: the Solomon Islands.

Most Japanese knew them for Guadalcanal, where lots of the heavy fighting took place during the war in the Pacific. These islands first appeared in Western history books in the sixteenth century when Spaniards discovered them, but oceanic peoples had been living there since at least one thousand BCE.

Most tourists visiting the islands were Japanese come to see the old battlegrounds, but in recent years their numbers had dwindled. It wasn't until four years ago that new ties were formed between Japan and the Solomon Islands with the construction of the Solomon Space Association on Maltide, a small island ringed with coral reefs and covered in jungle.

The SSA existed entirely on the funding of the OECF, Japan's Overseas Economic Cooperation Fund. The association's founder was one Isao Nasuda, a relatively unknown space enthusiast at the time. How he had managed to lobby his way into a position of such power was still something of a mystery.

"As part of our overseas development aid, we need to provide the Solomon Islands with broadcast education and a complete communications network," he had argued. "And the best way to do that is with communication satellites.

"Building dams and bridges is all very well and good, but if we build them and don't provide for their upkeep properly, we get burned by the critics. Maintaining a communications satellite network is no different, and it costs a hefty amount of money."

Everything up to this point in Nasuda's argument was pretty standard fare. It was the next part that upped the ante.

"In order to pull this off at the lowest possible price point, we need to deploy a manned spaceflight support network."

Nasuda was nothing if not self-serving.

Anyone with the least bit of experience in space development would have seen through his ploy in a moment. What he was suggesting was akin to building a factory in order to fix a flat tire on a bicycle. However, thanks to the uninformed officials hearing his case, the program had passed with no objections. Of course, what Nasuda really wanted was to realize low-cost manned spaceflight in order to seize a piece of the growing pie that was the global space industry.

Due to a general lack of media interest in foreign aid efforts, construction on the base had begun without the slightest reaction from taxpayers. Development of an entirely proprietary manned spaceflight system was soon under way. Everything was going swimmingly until plans stalled during the testing phase of their large-scale booster rocket. Nasuda had just received official notice that he had six months left to realize manned flight or the entire thing would be scrapped. That was right about the time Yukari Morita visited the island.

With a single, lightweight pilot like her in the orbiter, they might just be able to get away with the small-scale rockets they had already developed. Finding the similarly built Matsuri for a backup crew had just been icing on the cake.

In the end, they were able to send someone into space before their deadline, and the SSA survived. Not only that, but they were able to realize such a dramatic cost improvement that Nasuda's lie had transformed into a truth of sorts overnight. They had realized his vision of a manned space-repair service. Now the eyes of the world were on the SSA.

It was after this that they rolled out the MOB2 series of multiple-seat orbiters. However, they were still obliged to use the smallest astronauts possible. By reducing the weight of a crewmember by a single kilogram, they could shave all of seventy from the total weight of the rockets. By limiting crew height to 155 cm, they could reduce the weight of the orbiter alone by a whole seven hundred kilograms.

Which is how the future of the SSA came to rely on short, female pilots. Of which at present, they had only two. Two pilots to NASA's five hundred...

Five days after the orbiter's emergency splashdown in Yokohama.

The top staff were gathered in the meeting room on the third floor of the main SSA building for a roundup of the last mission.

"...Luckily, the soy sauce and vinegar compound did little damage to the cockpit controls. All of the electronic components are shielded, of course, to resist the effects of a small amount of moisture," chief engineer Hiroyuki Mukai reported. "As long as nothing seeps in through the outer hull."

"What about the momentary loss of power due to water damage? Is that something we should work on improving?" Kazuya Kinoshita asked. Kinoshita was the number two man at the SSA.

"I doubt there's any need. After splashdown, it doesn't really matter what breaks."

"Well, as long as the fuel cells don't explode."

"Which is why they jettison them before splashdown."

"But Yukari likes hanging on to them," Kinoshita noted. "Fuel cells make for a lot more power once you're on the ground. You can operate the air conditioning and use the radio without worrying about your batteries."

"Well, we'll just have to train her not to expect those luxuries."

"That's a possibility," Asahikawa noted. She was the chief medical officer in charge of every aspect of the astronauts' daily lives. "But there are limits. Actually, the problem with Yukari is she's been trained so well, she's starting to look for shortcuts to everything."

The room filled with laughter.

"Who would've thought that following fashions and studying for school tests would prepare someone so well for a career as an astronaut? Memorizing an orbiter manual is nothing to a homework-hardened schoolgirl," Nasuda said.

"Let's not underestimate Matsuri, either. Recall that she was somehow able to smuggle an entire durian into that capsule."

"How did she do that, anyway? We checked that capsule completely before liftoff," Mukai asked. He had been responsible for the prelaunch check.

"Apparently, she used a sort of hypnosis. By placing the inspection crew under a kind of trance, she made them unable to physically see the durian."

"Excuse me? Is that even possible?"

"I can't see any other way that she could have pulled it off. The Taliho tribe claims to have been doing this sort of thing for thousands of years, after all."

Satsuki had already debriefed the inspection crew. She had even tried hypnosis on them herself to get to the bottom of what had happened just before the rocket took off—but no clear answers were forthcoming.

"But wait," Mukai cut in. "If they can do that, why don't the Taliho all go off and make a killing robbing banks?"

"Let's just be grateful that they seem to have wisdom in equal amounts to their power. Mind you, I'm going to keep Matsuri confined to quarters until we're ready to strap her in next time."

"What happens if she hypnotizes the guards at her door?" Satsuki frowned.

"We just have to trust them, both of them," Nasuda said. "Thankfully, the durian did no real damage, and Yukari jettisoned the fuel cells as she was supposed to. If you don't mind, I'd like to discuss the malfunction in the sequencer next."

"Malfunction? You make it sound like there was something wrong with the electronics." Mukai snorted. "What happened was, Yukari left the protective cover on the activation switch open while she was dealing with the goldfish, and she accidentally bumped the switch. Yukari says so herself, and that account fits the telemetry records."

"So it was operator error."

"Not that I blame her. Everything happened with incredibly bad timing," Kinoshita said. "What Yukari is saying is that we can't have one person doing two jobs up there. Well, I suppose it's two people doing two jobs, but both of them are supposed to be checking the other's operations, so when you add an experiment to their list of duties, it's too much. They get confused."

"So they need a third person?" Nasuda crossed his arms.

Everyone in the room was aware that on the U.S. space shuttle, duties were divided between mission specialists and payload specialists.

"How is development going on the three-person orbiter?"

"As smoothly as could be wished for. All we're basically doing is cramming another seat into the MOB2 transport locker space."

"The trick is finding a mission specialist with the same dimensions as Yukari and Matsuri."

"No kidding. Whoever it is, they'll have to cram into a space barely fifty centimeters across."

[ACT 2]

"YOU KNOW WHAT we really need here? A disco."

It was lunch break. Yukari and Matsuri were sitting in the shade of a palm tree along the beach, sipping coconut milk.

"*Hoi?* What's a disco?"

"It's a place for young people to get together and dance and drink and stuff like that."

"Sounds like a sing-sing."

"What's that?"

"That's where everyone sings and dances, and men choose good women. The women decorate themselves and shake their hips and busts to attract the men. Oh, it's lots of fun."

"Erm...I guess that sounds similar," Yukari agreed, a vivid image rising in her mind of tribal people in a circle, beating on drums. "My point is, if we're going to try to get another high school girl out on this island, we need a disco, at least. You saw what it was like in Yokohama, right? There are boutiques and accessory shops and fast food and all kinds of stuff like that. Here, there's, well, this!"

Yukari gestured across the scene in front of them.

Palm trees. White sand. Coral reefs. The South Pacific.

"Sure, it's beautiful when you first get here, but the 'ooh' factor only lasts a couple days. No one is going to stay here long if there isn't a real potential for sustained fun, you know what I mean?"

"But you're here, Yukari."

"I don't have anyplace to go home to."

"*Hoi?*"

"I got kicked out of school, remember?"

"Oh." Matsuri made a sort of confused half smile. She reached down and pulled something resembling a rockfish, baked whole, from beside their little campfire. "Perfectly done!" she declared.

"Yeah."

Matsuri took a bite of the fish and passed it to Yukari.

It didn't taste bad once you got used to it, but boy did she miss the pizza back in Yokohama. Yukari checked the Omega Speedmaster on her left wrist. Lunch break would be over soon. "Guess we should be heading back."

Yukari slipped a light jacket on over her swimsuit and pressed the button on her transceiver. "Hi there, security? Pick up, please."

"Roger. We're on our way."

A short while later, a Humvee appeared down the beach. Using base security as a taxi service was one of the perks of being an astronaut.

With the entire future of the SSA resting on their shoulders, Yukari and Matsuri could get away with quite a bit. As long as they had a reasonable excuse, they could take chopper rides to the Chinatown on the other side of the island and use the private Gulfstream jet to go shopping in Australia. If they tried to pull a stunt like that as public officials in Japan, there would have been a firestorm of criticism, but here where the media rarely trod, there was no one to watch them.

The people on base called it "Solomon sickness": a feeling that grew with time spent on the islands that it was okay to do whatever you liked as long as you could get away with it. It was a pretty pleasant condition, as sicknesses went.

The Humvee drove past the launch platform and onto the two-kilometer-long road that went straight from the launching pad to the vehicle assembly building.

The white, crushed-coral pavement shimmered in the heat. Palm trees stood to either side of the road, like some ritzy boulevard in an exotic city—but here there was no one else but them.

The CB radio on the dashboard squawked.

"Car 5, Car 5, what's your current position?"

"Just passed the VAB, over."

"Mind stopping by the front gate? We've got a visitor there who won't budge."

"Roger that."

The driver returned his radio mic back to the dashboard and said to Yukari, "Sounds like we're going to take a little detour if that's all right."

"Sure. What's this 'visitor who won't budge' all about?"

"Probably a local taro-root salesman. They're pretty persistent."

"You think?"

Up ahead, a red-and-white striped crossing bar came into view. Off to the right of the road stood a small guard post and a stand of the broad-leaved tropical trees that grew all over the island.

Yukari spotted two people in the shade of the trees.

One, standing, was clearly a security guard, and the other—probably the visitor—was sitting on the ground. She wore a skirt, and her head hung slumped down between pale white shoulders. A wide-brimmed hat covered her face from view.

The Humvee stopped and the guard walked over to them. "It's a girl. Just arrived here by taxi. Seems like she got a little carsick—that is, the driver tells me that by the time she arrived at the port in Sanchago, she was already half-dead with motion sickness. I doubt the ride here made it any better."

When civilians visited the island, they had to take a rusty old ferry that left once every three days from Guadalcanal. Once they arrived, they had to take the sole taxi on the island over the mountains along twenty kilometers of dirt road. Anyone who wasn't riding in a Humvee or other vehicle made for off-roading was in for a nightmarish trip in the "taxi," which in this case was a makeshift collection of scrapped Datsun parts that might as well have had a bumper sticker reading Auto-mobile inspection? What's that?

The security guard jumped out of the Humvee and knelt in front of the girl. Her hat shifted and she looked up, revealing her face.

Yukari practically leapt out of the car. "Akane! What in the name—"

Akane Miura's eyes swam up to Yukari. "Well," she croaked, "I'm here."

"I can see you're here! But why?"

"I thought...I thought I might become an astronaut."

"For real? But what about school?"

"I dropped out. There's no going back," she said, her head slumping forward again.

[ACT 3]

AFRAID THAT ASAHIKAWA would start endurance tests on the girl if they took her to the infirmary, Yukari decided instead to take Akane to her own room in the dormitory. Once Akane had lain down on the bed and drunk some water, the color returned to her cheeks and she seemed to recover a bit.

"You still alive?" Yukari asked.

"Mostly." Akane slowly sat up.

Yukari and Matsuri brought chairs up to the bedside and joined her. Yukari offered her some coconut milk with tapioca, but Akane didn't seem interested.

Her stomach's still turning somersaults.

"I have to admit, this is a complete surprise."

"I'm sorry. I thought that if I called, you might tell me not to come."

"No need to apologize. I'm really happy you're here."

"Really?" Akane said.

"Really. You're the first person I actually invited, you know."

"Oh. Well, that's a relief." A smile like a spring sunbeam spread across Akane's face.

"You really dropped out of school?"

"Yeah."

Akane began to relate the tale of how the principal and the guidance counselor had chewed her out. At first, Yukari had just sighed inwardly, but as Akane went on, she felt her anger growing.

"They just kept repeating that it's against the rules to leave school while class is in session. I couldn't believe they didn't seem to care at all about the goldfish."

"Man, what's with that guy? He's always like that!"

"Here I was saving the goldfish and making a contribution to science, and they treated me like I was some kind of delinquent." Akane was getting angry too. "Teachers shouldn't do that."

"Yeah, he should be the one getting kicked out!"

"So I let him have it."

"All right! You go girl!"

"I told him I would leave school for a while to see what I might be able to learn in the outside world."

The wind dropped out of Yukari's sails.

"I've never lost my temper before then," Akane said, still excited. "I think I even surprised myself."

That was an awfully rational thing for someone losing their temper to say, Yukari thought, but what she said was, "Didn't your parents object?"

"Oh, they were totally against it." Akane stuck out her tongue. (Yukari: *Ha! Cute!*) "So I went on a hunger strike for three days in my room, and finally my father said he would 'give me a year to figure things out.' They agreed to just pretend I'd gotten sick or something."

"Whatever works."

"Well, I'm not sure what's going to happen a year from now. I'm not sure what I'll learn, either."

"Don't worry, I'm sure you can get an extension," Matsuri said, joining the conversation. "Yukari was only going to be here for half a year at first, you know."

"Hey!" Yukari frowned.

"Of course," Akane said, "I don't know if they'll hire me yet or not."

"Both of us will vouch for you!" Yukari said, grinning. "They'll take you for sure."

"I'm not very tough..."

"Leave that to us!" Yukari grabbed Akane by the hands. "We're not going to let you fail, got it? I'm taking you to space, promise!"

"Yukari..." Tears shone in Akane's eyes. "Thank you."

"You can thank me after liftoff."

Akane nodded. "So, this seems kind of funny to ask now, but how do I apply to become an astronaut?"

"There's no real set procedure. I guess talking to the director would be the quickest route. Can you walk?"

"I think so..." Akane stood, a little shaky, and stepped away from the bed.

Yukari picked up an intercom and punched in the number for the director's office. "It's Yukari. We have an applicant here. Right...the genius girl who saved the goldfish. Okay." She set down the receiver. "They'll see you at once."

Akane nodded and gulped.

Nasuda's office was about as far away, décor-wise, as you could get from the principal's office at Nellis Academy. There wasn't a single bit of adornment in the place. It was all steel desks piled with documents, a dry-erase board, bookshelves, and an old coffee maker with some chipped cups for guests. With the exception of the large photo of a rocket hanging on the wall, it could have been an office in any small company.

A man and a woman sat at the desk across from the door.

The man was in his sixties, bald save for a small patch of hair at the very top of his head and intensely black eyebrows. A wild light in his eyes shone through round, silver-rimmed glasses.

The woman was no older than thirty. She had rich black hair and wore a lab coat over a tight miniskirt. Red high heels stuck out from beneath the desk, a spot of color in the otherwise drab office.

The aging boss and his trophy secretary, Yukari thought. *As if.*

Nasuda spoke first. "Thanks for coming. I'm Nasuda, the director here. My associate is our chief medical examiner, Satsuki Asahikawa. She's in charge of astronaut training and health maintenance."

"Akane Miura," Akane introduced herself, bowing so low her hair fell down over the top of her head. "I've come to apply for the position of astronaut."

"We've heard about you from Yukari. Sounds like you did quite well for those goldfish."

"It was nothing," she began, then hastily added, "that is, I think that if I became an astronaut, I could make myself very useful in a variety of situations."

"I see." Nasuda glanced over at Satsuki.

She leaned closer to him and whispered in his ear. "Thirty-six kilos."

"Measurements?"

"Height, 153 centimeters. Her measurements are seventy-four, fifty-two, seventy-five."

"No complaints here, then."

"Don't jump to conclusions. I'm worried about her stamina."

"Right."

It was a remarkable talent of Satsuki's that she could glance at a person and immediately gauge their weight, size, and general level of fitness.

"Miss Miura, thank you for coming all this way," Nasuda said, turning back to their applicant. "I'm sure you're tired from your trip, so we'll begin the examinations tomorrow."

"Okay."

"Satsuki will be taking care of you while you're here. Our medical examination can be a little hard at times, but hang in there. We'll put you up at the guesthouse. Don't get excited, it's just a room, and pretty plain at that. That okay?"

"That will be fine." She turned to Satsuki. "I look forward to working with you, ma'am."

"Likewise, Akane," Satsuki replied, a mischievous smile on her lips.

I guess it wasn't quite as easy as I thought it would be, Yukari thought. For her and Matsuri getting a job had been as simple as walking in the building. Now she was starting to worry. *I really hope they take her.*

[ACT 4]

THE ASTRONAUT TRAINING center was a three-story building off to one side of the main complex.

There Akane spent the entire following day. It was not long into her medical exam that Akane realized just how powerful Satsuki Asahikawa was—at least here, in her own domain.

She measured Akane's height, her weight, her chest size, her inseam, gripping power, eyesight, ability to distinguish colors, hearing, lung capacity—so far, nothing was all that different from a standard health exam, if a bit more rushed.

Then Satsuki stripped her down to her underwear, put

a respiration mask on her mouth, placed electrodes all over her body, and put her on an ergometer, which was something like an exercise bicycle. She ran out of breath after ten minutes. After thirty minutes, she felt dizzy and slumped over the handlebars.

"What's wrong?" Satsuki asked, a look of despair on her face. "Giving up so soon?"

Akane swallowed. "N-no, of course not. I'm...I'm fine."

"Really? You're really fine?"

"Yes. Yes, I'm fine."

"You're really *really* sure you're fine?"

"Yes, I'm perfectly fine!" Akane forced a smile.

"That's what I like to hear!" Satsuki narrowed her eyes. "Next up is the decompression chamber, I think."

Practically skipping with excitement, Satsuki led Akane into another room.

This room was shaped like a cylindrical tube, with just enough space for a person to walk in a circle. The walls were made of thick stainless steel.

"In here we can adjust the air pressure however we want in order to test your adaptability. I'll have you sit down, and I'll leave the room, but you can talk to me on the intercom there. If you feel like you can't take it anymore, just tell me. You'll also have a dead-man's switch—but remember, stick it out as long as you can or you won't have much hope of becoming an astronaut."

The deadman's switch was held in the right hand. She was supposed to press down the button and keep it down. Were she to lose consciousness, her thumb would lift off the switch and alert the controller, and the pressure would normalize.

Akane went into the chamber and sat down on the lone chair.

"You're all set. Good luck!"

"Thanks."

Behind her, the heavy steel hatch shut with a *thunk*. There was a small round porthole through which Akane could watch

Satsuki at the controls.

She's enjoying this.

Akane recollected what Yukari and Matsuri had told her about the chief medical examiner the night before.

"Keep a close eye on Satsuki," Yukari warned her. "She can be vicious."

Matsuri nodded emphatically.

"I did a lot of training for track, and Matsuri grew up here in the jungle, so we both made it through, but it wasn't easy."

"How so?" Akane asked.

"Oh, I must have lost consciousness five or six times total."

Akane was confused. "Wait, but it's a medical examination, right?"

"In theory."

"What is it really then?"

"Human experimentation. She wants to see just how much we can take."

Akane sighed.

"As soon as Satsuki sees you can take whatever she's dishing out, she escalates."

"What exactly are we talking about here?"

Yukari went through the various trials in explicit, grueling detail.

Akane felt the blood drain from her face. "Is there like a minimum required performance on each test? A score you have to get or you fail?"

"That's what she won't tell you. Not even if you ask."

"Then how am I supposed to prepare?" Akane was starting to panic. She had a great deal of confidence when it came to written tests, but she had never taken a test where she didn't even know how she was being scored. Let alone a test you had to pass with your body, not your mind.

"There is a psychological aspect to it too, right, Matsuri?"

"That's right. When Satsuki puts you through the rounds, it's like she's wearing a mask."

"A mask...?"

"Nothing to worry about," Matsuri said, unconvincingly. "Just tell the truth. She'll know if you're lying."

Akane sighed again.

"Right," Yukari agreed. "Better to just focus on how you're doing and not pay attention to Satsuki at all."

"All right..."

"Not much else we can do, really," Yukari admitted.

"Nope, there isn't," Matsuri said.

"Well, I'll try my best."

Akane heard a thrumming sound, like a vacuum pump whirring to life.

Her ears had begun to hurt.

She swallowed and felt her ears pop.

Calm down. Calm down.

"How do you feel?"

"All right."

So far this isn't half as bad as I thought it was going to be from the way they were talking last night, Akane thought.

Satsuki's face wasn't a mask. In fact, she seemed genuinely happy for Akane's progress. She wondered what it meant.

"Air pressure, as you know, is inversely proportional to altitude. Just now, you went up to two thousand meters above sea level. I'm going to bring you back down to the surface, and next we're going to go up to five thousand."

"All right."

Air pressure returned, and then the decompression started again.

Akane kept up, though she had to pop her ears several times.

"Some people forget to pop and their ears bleed. Just remember to keep popping them and you'll be all right," Yukari had warned her.

"Question: what is the altitude of Mt. Ararat?"

"Um...5,165 meters?"

"You are a grade-A student. Well, you're standing on the peak now. How do you feel?"

Akane had developed a headache a short while earlier. She could feel the pain increasing with each passing moment.

"Um...I'm okay."

"Really?"

"Really. I'm doing fine."

"You're not pushing it? You're really absolutely fine?"

"I'm absolutely positively doing great."

"Then let's take you up to Annapurna. Or do you want to pass?"

Yukari would have taken that as a direct challenge, no doubt. But Akane saw it differently. She didn't want to let Satsuki down.

"I'm ready."

The sound of the pump grew louder.

How high was Annapurna again? Eight-thousand-something meters?

Her head throbbed with pain, and she could feel her thoughts begin to drift. Her breathing was ragged. It seemed to take forever until she heard Satsuki over the intercom announce in a singsong voice, "You made it! Welcome to Annapurna! One more question: which integer has a square root closest in value to the base of the natural logarithm?"

Huh...what? A math question? The base of the natural logarithm? Uh, what was base e again? 2.71828...

If the root of 8 is 2.82...and 7 is...uh...7 is...

Akane tried to focus her thoughts through her splitting headache, but she still couldn't come up with the root of seven.

Wait, if I square e, then take the root of the right side of the equation...

Seven...7...7...49!

"S...seven. It's seven."

"Impressive. Ready to come down again?"

The sound of the pump quieted and the air pressure began to return.

"The terminal velocity of an orbiter during reentry is two hundred kilometers per second. If you ever wanted to know what would happen if you lost pressure on reentry, you're experiencing it now. High mountain climbers don't have it nearly this rough."

She popped her ears again. By now she couldn't tell whether the pain was coming from her ears or her headache, so she kept popping them as quickly as she could, just in case. When the air pressure returned to surface levels, the hatch opened.

Akane's head still throbbed. Shaky on her feet, she stepped out, when a wave of nausea came over her and she had to drop to a crouch.

Two red-enamel high heels came into her tear-blurred field of vision. "Oh? What's wrong? Giving up?"

She looked up to see that now-familiar look of despair in Satsuki's eyes. Had she failed the test already? Had she not lived up to expectations?

"N-no, I'm fine."

"Really now? Are you sure? You look pale."

"No, really. I'm okay."

"Are you really, really okay?"

"Yes. Perfectly. Great." Akane summoned the last of her strength and managed a half smile.

"That a girl!" Satsuki grinned. "Next up, how about a little centrifuge?"

Satsuki giggled.

[ACT 5]

"YUKARI? OH, YUKARI? You with me?"

Yukari shook her head. She'd been daydreaming. "Sorry, Chief."

She was standing in the orbiter clean room in a corner of the VAB.

"If you don't fully understand what we've changed, it'll come back to bite you up there," chief engineer Mukai explained. "As you know, we try to get the most out of our crew, since we're spending all this money to get you up there. There is not a lot of redundancy in your onboard systems. If a main panel goes down and the backup stops, you'll have to fix it yourself on the spot."

"I know that."

"You worried about something? You seem distracted."

"Well, maybe. A little."

"Yukari's afraid Akane won't pass the examination," Matsuri explained.

"Satsuki running that?" he asked.

"Yeah."

Mukai started nodding to himself. "Of course, of course. That explains *that*."

"Explains what?"

"I've been having dips in power here at the factory since this morning. I was wondering what was going on."

"You mean like power shortages?"

"Yeah, like something on base was using a lot of power all at once—something outside of the VAB."

"Like what?"

"Probably Satsuki's centrifuge. Running that thing at full power uses up as much wattage as a small city."

"Running it at full power?"

Terrifying memories of her own time in the centrifuge rose in Yukari's mind. The centrifuge was like a giant merry-go-round for one, except you didn't ride on a horse, you rode inside an airtight box. The box could be positioned in any way, meaning that the person inside was subjected to centrifugal force from every direction.

Yukari had been run through the device soon after agreeing to become an astronaut. On her first run, a full 9 G pressing on her chest had squeezed the breath out of her and she had fainted. And Satsuki gave it to you easy from the front. You could take a lot more G from the top.

Satsuki hadn't given her any warning when she was going to change the direction, either, until Yukari felt like a rag doll in a dryer. Her internal organs bounced around like pinballs inside her, and she lost count of the times she fainted only to wake up covered in her own vomit. Once the pressure had been so bad, Yukari had felt her shoulder nearly dislocate. Depending on the speed at which the device rotated, the G could be pushed up to a limit of thirty times normal Earth gravity. This meant that a body weighing forty kilograms would feel thirty times heavier. At weights like that, most people died in a very short amount of time.

And now Satsuki was whipping poor Akane around at full power?

Yukari's face went pale. "Mukai, sorry, but can I take a quick break?"

"But—" Mukai began, then he sighed. He knew he wouldn't be able to stop her when she was like this. Mukai was younger than most of the other scientists on base and not as good at resisting the whims of their astronauts.

"Fine. See you soon."

Yukari dashed out of the clean room, jumped out of her coveralls, and ran for the training center. She could hear motors spinning as soon as she stepped inside.

The centrifuge was in the basement.

Yukari ran down the stairs, taking two steps at a time. Throwing open the door to the centrifuge control room, she barged in, shouting, "Stop the machine! You can't throw her on full power! She'll die!"

"Huh?" Satsuki was standing with the back of her white lab coat to the door. She turned around. "Oh, no one's in the centrifuge. I hadn't used it for a while, so I was just warming it up."

"What...?" Yukari gave a deep sigh, but she wasn't done quite yet. "Where's Akane?"

"I'm giving her a break. She should be here any moment now."

"How's she doing?"

"Far better than I expected, actually."

"Really?" Yukari found herself smiling.

"Yes. In fact, all she has to clear is the centrifuge and I think we have a winner."

Yukari's smile faded. "How many G are you going to put her through?"

"I won't know until I start, now will I. That's why we have this test, you know."

"As I recall, you ran me until I passed out several times. Including taking me from nothing to 9 G right off the bat. How fast are you taking her?"

"Like I said, I won't know until we begin."

"Admit it! You just like torturing us with your machines!"

Satsuki lifted an eyebrow. "What's gotten under your collar?"

"I'm just saying, the orbiter seats two now so it only goes up to 8 G instead of ten like it used to. Why take her farther than she needs to?"

"The specifications of that rocket and the aptitude tests are two different things. If I don't know for certain how much this girl can take, I won't know how suited she is for the job, and I won't be able to create an appropriate training schedule for her."

"Well that may be so, but..." Yukari's objection trailed off.

"Yukari. I know I might not look it sometimes, but I am a medical doctor. And yes, I might come off a little crazy, but I promise I'll stop at the last possible moment."

"That's what I'm talking about! Why do you have to go up to the last possible moment?"

Just then, Akane walked in, wearing a gym shirt. Her face looked gaunt, and her feet were dragging.

"Yukari? What are you doing here?"

"I was negotiating. I'm trying to save you from this torture."

"You don't have to worry about me, really. I'm doing the best I can. I want to pass this test."

"That's all well and good, but you just wait until she starts taunting you. There's no telling what she'll have you doing. Human experimentation, that's what this is!"

Satsuki rolled her eyes. "Must you always say that?"

"Eight G, tops!" Yukari glared at her. "As your primary astronaut I'm giving you my expert opinion. Take her up to 8 G from the front, and no higher!"

"Only 8 G?"

"You heard me. That's plenty with our current booster!" She glared at Satsuki again for effect.

Satsuki frowned and glared back at the shorter Yukari, but it was Satsuki who broke away first.

"Fine. But don't get the idea that everything you say goes here." Satsuki turned a dial on her console and the centrifuge spun down. "Maybe you could help Akane into the cage?"

Yukari nodded quietly. "Let's go, Akane. Can you walk?"

"Sure..."

Yukari lent the other girl her shoulder and together they left the control room. Down a short staircase, they entered a room shaped like an elliptical pool, with the centrifuge at its center. The centrifuge had a central column and a long arm, at the end of which hung the cage. Yukari opened the cage door and helped Akane inside. She tightened a four-point harness around Akane's chest and then strapped her in at the waist and legs.

"It might be a little tight, but trust me, you'll prefer it that way."

"Okay."

Yukari checked all the fastenings carefully. A simple slip from your chair at high G could mean broken bones.

"See those buttons on the panel in front of you? Some of them will light up, and you'll be instructed to press them."

"Okay."

"Over 4 G and it gets hard just to raise your arm, but as long as you remember to breathe with your stomach, you shouldn't faint."

"Okay."

"Good luck. You know, Satsuki said you were doing really well."

"I am? Really?"

"Yeah. She said if you pass this, you've made it."

"I won't let you down, Yukari."

"I know you won't. I'll be watching from the control room, okay?"

Yukari shut the cage door and went back upstairs.

Satsuki was talking to Akane over the intercom. "Akane? Can you hear me?"

"Loud and clear."

"Did Yukari tell you about the buttons?"

"I'm supposed to press the ones that light up, right?"

"That's right. We're going to be testing your judgment and physical capacity at heavier gravities. Here goes."

Satsuki began flipping switches, murmuring to herself, "Rotation floor clear, activating motors..."

The centrifuge began to spin.

Satsuki glanced down at the reading on the console. "Two G. How do you feel?"

"*O...okay.*"

Yukari glanced at the doctor's face. Satsuki was expressionless. Her manicured fingers slowly clicked the dial controlling rotation speed.

"Three G. Is something wrong? You're a little slow on the buttons."

"Ah...suh...sorry." Akane's voice over the intercom sounded pained.

Yukari clenched her fists. *Hang in there, Akane. Even an accelerating sports car will give you 3 G. The rocket will give you eight. Come on, please be able to take 8 G.*

"Four G. We are approaching realistic levels now. How do you feel?"

No answer.

"Akane? What's wrong?"

Akane didn't respond.

Come on, Akane! Answer!

"Maybe the intercom's malfunctioning." Satsuki pressed the stop button. As soon as the centrifuge had wound down, Yukari and Satsuki ran down to the cage.

Satsuki lifted the latch and looked inside. The two stared at each other in silence. Akane was out cold.

She hadn't even made it past 4 G.

[ACT 6]

"IT'S OKAY, YOU don't have to apologize so much."

"I'm so sorry..."

Akane was lying in bed, gazing vacantly at the ceiling. She hugged a teddy bear tight to her chest. It was one of the few things she had brought with her from Japan.

Yukari and Matsuri sat next to the bed like visitors in a hospital ward.

"There's no way they're going to take me. I fainted at 4 G! I'm done."

"Don't worry, you'll get better with training—"

"But there won't be any training if they don't accept me. You made it to 9 G, didn't you, Yukari?"

"Well yeah, but—"

"What about you, Matsuri?"

"*Hoi!* My first time I made it to 17 G."

Akane turned to face the wall.

"Don't worry, Matsuri's kind of a special case," Yukari explained. "She's like a female Tarzan or something. You could shoot her in the head and she wouldn't even die."

"Yukari?" Akane whispered.

"Yeah?"

"You don't want to go on a mission with someone who faints during takeoff, do you?"

"Well, I..." There was a pause. "I don't mind! Not a bit. There's nothing to do during takeoff anyway—the first time I was up there all by myself. Besides, I could just wake you up once we were in orbit. No problem."

"You don't have to say that just to make me feel better," Akane said quietly.

Yukari was starting to get frustrated. "Matsuri! Can't you cast a spell or something to raise her spirits?"

"She needs to sleep," Matsuri said simply. "Have a good rest, Akane. You're exhausted, so it should come easy."

"Yeah..."

"Okay. I guess that's it for tonight, then." Yukari stood, feeling slightly relieved. "Good night."

"Good night..."

[ACT 7]

"THERE ARE NO issues with her physique or sensory organs. Personality wise, she's very warm and takes instruction well, and has a great sense of responsibility. She is quite intelligent to boot and can focus under stress. She's also stronger than I expected. The only problem is her lack of any high-G resilience." Satsuki Asahikawa was giving her report at the director's meeting the following day.

"So she can't take the gravity? Is that an automatic fail?" Nasuda asked, getting right to the point.

"She passed out the moment I took her up to four. With that low a resilience, she couldn't even ride a roller coaster."

"What? Only 4 G?"

"Too bad. Her scholastic ability is off the charts," Kinoshita said, relating his impressions from the interview. "Actually, rather than scholastic ability I should say her general comprehension. I presented her with several trick questions and she was very good at cutting through the chaff and getting right to the point. She's able to see the true nature of the problem at hand, understand it, and act on it."

"Yes, but 4 G?" Satsuki raised her hands. "Our astronauts are subjected to at least 8 G during liftoff and reentry. If she's fainting at a mere four, she simply won't be able to perform her duties as a member of the flight crew."

"Can't something be done about that in training?"

Satsuki shook her head. "It's not just that she has to stay conscious at 8 G. She has to be able to assess her situation, make split-second decisions, and take *action* at 8 G. If we are only talking about a consciousness threshold, I'd want her to stay awake up to at least 10 G."

Nasuda groaned. "Let me just confirm, you're saying there is zero probability that she would be able to perform in a real-life situation?"

"Well, I wouldn't say zero," Satsuki admitted with a frown.

"Yukari has told us several times, and we know this ourselves, that they need a division of labor while in orbit. Our lack of that is one big reason we haven't been able to get the thumbs-up from NASA. And there's something else." Nasuda reached into his briefcase and pulled out a single sheet of paper. He showed it to everyone at the table.

It was a printout of a photograph showing five girls, blondes and brunettes, standing in a row, smiling.

"This was up on the CNES homepage as of yesterday. Turns out a subsidiary of Arianespace in France has started a project called the 'Ariane Courier.' They're not ready for commercial flights, but the plan is for them to put small astronauts in a small orbiter and provide services like satellite repair."

"They're totally copying us!" Mukai said, aghast.

"We knew we'd have some competition. I just didn't imagine they would pop up so quickly. They're going to be using an Ariane 4 rocket modified to carry people."

"What about space suits? Do they have skintight suits yet?"

"We don't think so. I'm guessing what they're wearing in that picture are just leotards. They're attractive though, aren't they, Kinoshita."

"Sadly, yes. Though our own girls are nothing to sneeze at."

Kinoshita was a man of encyclopedic knowledge in many fields, one of them being the media market for attractive girls. And this, of course, was a cornerstone of the SSA's business strategy.

While previous astronauts had served as flag carriers for their nation's pride, they were now often used as PR tools for getting taxpayers behind a project. An operation like the SSA depended heavily on goodwill toward Yukari and Matsuri for their continued funding. Their appeal to the folks back home was the only thing between the SSA and a firestorm over the massive amounts of taxpayer money disappearing into their project.

"However, going up against five girls in the prime of their youth—that's tough competition."

"Absolutely. Looks aside, the biggest problem here is that there are already five of them," Nasuda said. "Really, we should have a main team and a backup team by now. If we're running with a two-person orbiter, we need at least four astronauts. If we've got a three-seater, I'd want at least six. And all we have is two. No wonder NASA doesn't trust us. If one of our astronauts caught a cold, our launch would be delayed."

"So you want numbers over quality, is that it?" Satsuki asked.

"Honestly, yes. I mean, even in the worst-case scenario, if Akane did pass out, one of the others could wake her up, couldn't they?"

"Well I'm against it! Even if we do have a three-seat orbiter, the majority of our launches will be with only two astronauts. If we're forced to rely on a sole astronaut during the most critical moments of takeoff and reentry because the other one is out cold, NASA will never trust us."

"Not if they don't know about it."

"Director!"

"Now now, Doctor—"

"Even if we disregard the issue of trust, we're talking about safety!" Satsuki slammed the table with her fists. "Imagine what would happen if those girls died? That *is* what I'm talking about when I say 'safety,' sir!"

The room was silent. After a few moments passed, Mukai spoke. "Satsuki, I think that goes without saying—"

"Apparently it doesn't."

"No. Everyone here knows that lives are on the line. But if we were to require one hundred percent safety before a launch, we'd never get off the ground. What we're all trying our very hardest to do here is to find an appropriate compromise between safety on one hand and the economic realities of the space industry on the other."

Satsuki turned to Mukai. "So you think that it's all right if one of them faints during liftoff?"

"I'm not saying that. But there are over two thousand sensors and a multitasking computer checking for abnormalities every millisecond of takeoff, as well as a fully automatic mechanism to separate the orbiter from the rest of the rocket. We can also remotely control much of the rocket from ground-based systems. Only when all of this fails is pilot action required."

"And yet it seems that every time we launch, our astronauts are surviving only by the skin of their teeth."

"Let me put it another way. If something truly catastrophic were to happen, like if the booster were to explode, then no number of safety measures and no amount of pilot skill would help them one bit. If we're going to let worry about that paralyze us, we need to scrap the program entirely. As an engineer, the only way I can sleep at night is because I know that we are doing everything we can here, on the ground, to prevent a worst-case scenario. We've had small difficulties with every launch, it's true, but no big accidents as of yet, right?"

Satsuki pondered the young technician's words.

"All right. I'm sorry for bringing up death. It just seemed like the elephant in the room. I understand what you're saying, but as the person ultimately responsible for the human factor in this equation, I cannot condone hiring Akane. My decision is final."

"What if we thought about it like this," Kinoshita offered. "It's true that the greatest risk on a flight comes with the launch and the reentry, but this only accounts for two percent of total flight time. And there's plenty of danger while in orbit."

"Your point?"

"Well, when I think about our easily excitable Yukari and our utterly unpredictable Matsuri, I can't help but think that a girl like Akane is the perfect complement to them. I think we could safely say that having her on board would dramatically improve safety for at least ninety-eight percent of the mission."

"So you want to hire her too?"

Kinoshita chuckled wryly. "This is outside my area of expertise as a physicist, but it's my impression that this girl makes up for in intellect what she lacks in physical strength. Here's my suggestion: we let her do a make-up test, except this time, we test her overall aptitude. Then we decide. How about it?"

"What exactly do you mean by an overall aptitude test?"

"Well..."

Kinoshita briefly explained what he was thinking.

"You're going to do *that* to her?" Satsuki was aghast.

"Yes. Completely solo. No support."

"She won't make it. Yukari was in pretty good shape, but who knows what would have happened to her if she hadn't run into Matsuri?"

"Well, we won't know that until we try, will we? If she passes, will you give her the okay, Satsuki?"

"I suppose I could take it under consideration."

"How about you, Director?"

"I suppose we could give it a shot." Then, Nasuda added, "Of course, it's going to be tricky to ensure she's completely without support."

[ACT 8]

"KNOCK KNOCK! GOOD morning, Akane!"

"*Hoi*, Akane! Wake-up time!"

For the past two days, Yukari and Matsuri had come each morning to Akane's room to take her to breakfast. She was always ready to go when they got there—except for today.

"*Hoi?* I don't think she's here."

"Akane? We're coming in."

Yukari turned the knob. It wasn't locked.

The room was completely empty. No suitcase, no jacket hanging on the wall, and no books on the desk. The bed showed no signs of having been slept in.

Yukari quickly ran back to the hallway and checked the number on the door. Room 201. This was the place.

The two girls went downstairs to the concierge. "Did Akane move to a different room?"

"Who? Miss Miura? Oh, you hadn't heard? She left yesterday."

"What do you mean 'left'?"

"I was told she was going back to Japan so she wouldn't be needing her room after yesterday."

"What? You mean she left without telling us?"

"That's odd. Didn't you three get along well? I wonder why she would have done that."

The concierge here made up for having no work to do by being nosy. Yukari left without another word. She went straight for the training center. Up the stairs, she found the door with the plate reading SPACE BIOLOGY LAB and went in without knocking.

Satsuki Asahikawa was inside, sitting in front of a tray with some toast and tomato juice on it, reading a trade magazine of some sort.

"Satsuki?"

"Yukari! Good morning."

"Is it true that Akane went back to Japan?"

"What? You didn't know? Yes, she went home yesterday."

"You mean, she failed the test."

Satsuki set down her magazine and shifted in her chair. "Unfortunately, yes. You were there, were you not? Someone who faints at 4 G just can't be an astronaut."

"But she could have gotten better with training!"

"Don't look at me like that. The testing is used to determine aptitude—the scope of a person's abilities at the present moment. Not in some hypothetical future."

"That may be, but she came all this way, she even quit school, and we just send her home?"

"Believe me, I didn't want to do it. But the job requires more than just dedication and enthusiasm," Satsuki said. "This is really the best for her, and for you and Matsuri. Please understand."

Yukari knew that laying this on Satsuki would get her nowhere, but it was still hard to accept. "Why did she leave without saying a word?"

"She was probably too embarrassed."

"Why?"

"Because you were the one who recommended her. In a sense, she failed *you*."

"She did nothing of the sort!" Yukari shouted. "I was the one who dragged her here! I was the one who told her she'd be hired in an instant, no problem. And she believed me. That's why she came. It's not her fault at all. It's mine!"

A fleck of spittle shot from Yukari's mouth and landed in Satsuki's glass of tomato juice, sending ripples across the surface. Satsuki held up her hands. "Okay, okay. I get it."

"It was my fault." Yukari's voice sounded strained.

"I understand."

"I thought she could help out. I thought she was a good fit. That's why I invited her."

"There's nothing wrong with that approach. Nothing at all," Satsuki said.

"And she was fine in the helicopter. She didn't get sick or faint."

"People get carsick for any number of reasons."

"And you should've seen the look in her eyes when I invited her to go up with me."

"Yukari—"

"I told her I wanted to show her the world from above. How beautiful it was."

"Yukari," Satsuki said, her voice gentle, "enough." Satsuki stood and walked over to Yukari's side. She pulled out a handkerchief and wiped the tears off her cheek.

"I don't even know why I'm crying," Yukari said with a sniffle.

"It's okay." She tapped Yukari lightly on the shoulder. "Here, have a seat."

Yukari sat down on a nearby bench.

"Look. She may have failed this time, but I think there's a possibility for a second chance. She's much more of a fighter than she seems at first."

Yukari rubbed her eyes with both hands and cried a bit more.

Satsuki watched her quietly.

At length, Yukari spoke. "Satsuki?"

"Yes?"

"Could you give me Akane's telephone number?"

"Her telephone number?"

"I want to call her and apologize."

"But you don't have anything to apologize for—"

"I don't want her to think it's her fault!"

"All right, all right." Satsuki thought for a second, then said, "You know...I don't think I ever asked for her phone number."

"What? Didn't she have to fill out any medical forms or anything?"

"That's the thing—I was thinking of doing that when she got hired."

"You don't have her address?"

"Not even that."

"I guess I could always dial information."

"Look, Yukari. I'm sure she's not home yet anyway. And maybe you want to wait a little while in any case. Give her a week at least."

"Why?"

"You both have a lot on your mind right now. You should let things settle a bit first. Then talk."

"You think?"

"Yes. Absolutely! That's my opinion as a doctor."

"Okay, then. That's what I'll do."

Yukari nodded, blew her nose, and went back out the door, leaving Satsuki to breathe a deep sigh of relief.

[ACT 9]

SUNDAY, SIX DAYS later.

With SSA rockets going up monthly, both the ground crew and astronauts rarely had a moment to breathe, but today was a rare pause from work for everybody.

Matsuri was decked out from head to toe in tribal garb—a bit misleading, since that tribal garb comprised little more than a bikini, and a small one at that.

What she lacked in skin coverage, though, she made up for with tropical bling: necklaces, bracelets, anklets—she had the works. Most were made from local flora and fauna, such as palm fronds, rattan fibers, exquisite seashells, and the fangs of small animals, but here and there could be spotted a stray bolt or washer she had picked up on base, or strips of glittery fabric cut from a thermal blanket. Each piece played a role in the local brand of magic, but clearly there was some flexibility in the tradition when it came to materials.

Most Taliho dressed far more austerely, but Matsuri was special. She had been tapped to be the next shaman of the tribe. She strode out through the main gate, a spear in her right hand and a woven hemp satchel in her left.

"Hey there, Matsuri," the guard called out to her. "Where are you headed?"

"To the northern jungle to gather *irippe* nuts. Might find a durian too, if I'm lucky."

"I'm afraid the jungle is off-limits right now."

"*Hoi?* The whole jungle? Why?"

"Security is doing live ammo training."

"But it's been nine years since we've been able to gather nuts in the north. I have to go now."

"Sorry, but off-limits is off-limits."

Matsuri frowned and walked over to the guard. She looked at him with her black eyes, like a cat's. She looked *through* him.

The guard's expression softened.

"Bullets won't hit me," Matsuri whispered.

"...Bullets won't hit you."

"I'll be fine."

"...You'll be fine."

"Open the gates."

"On it."

The guard pressed the large red button and the striped bar across the road lifted.

Matsuri grinned and walked through.

The Solomon Space Center had been built on several square kilometers of flat land carved out of the jungle on the eastern edge of the island.

Through the gate, the unpaved road was quickly swallowed by jungle. To the southwest, the jungle rose, becoming the jagged ridgeline of the Shiribas Range.

The dangers of these tropical jungles, be it the blistering heat, fanged beasts and giant snakes, malaria, or cannibals, were often exaggerated to near mythical heights. In truth, it did get hot and steamy between the trees at times, but the ick-factor was really no different from what one might feel during the rainy season in Japan. There were hardly any large animals, and all cannibalism had been stamped out by missionaries years ago. Nor did healthy people who had been properly inoculated need to worry much about malaria.

Though there was a constant struggle between the plants of the forest for nutrients and sunlight, the front lines in that battle were in the canopy. Hardly anything of size grew on the dimly lit jungle floor. The main barrier to getting around for anyone who hadn't grown up here was the thick tangle of low-lying broadleaf shrubs. Most of the shrubs sent out roots that popped up from the forest floor like shark fins, crisscrossing in all directions. The layered roots and vines, and fallen trees that lay like small mountains covered in moss, all served to restrict vision and slow travel by foot to a crawl.

Most of a traveler's energy was spent clambering up and down the various obstacles. Without a clear view of one's surroundings, it was impossible to avoid the natural barriers and barricades, and often inexperienced adventurers would find themselves at a dead end and forced to turn back. The experience could be so disheartening that, as the traveler's exhaustion deepened, some gave up trying to find a route, and instead lay down and simply wasted away.

A short distance down the road, Matsuri made a right angle and stepped into the forest. She continued walking, weaving between the trees, her pace no slower than it had been on the open road. She walked like a cat, making not a sound, stirring not a leaf. It was almost as if she swam through the foliage, so at home did she seem there.

It was nearing noon when she reached her destination.

"*Hoi!*" she exclaimed in a reverent whisper. "Beautiful!"

An endless stream of small nuts fell from the canopy, twirling in the air as they made their way to the forest floor. When they crossed the path of the few sunbeams that penetrated the canopy, they glittered and sparkled in the air.

On the ground, the brownish winged nuts looked like badminton shuttlecocks. Matsuri knelt to pick some of them up. She removed and discarded the wings, leaving only the nut, which she placed in her satchel. The nuts lay strewn about everywhere. Matsuri barely had to move in order to keep gathering. The more nuts she picked up, the more came twirling down.

Irippe nuts were very rich in oil and one of Matsuri's favorite foods. Yet they flowered so rarely—only once every several years, and sometimes not for decades—that if you weren't careful, you might miss them altogether. The Taliho called these times when the irippe fell "nut years" because for various ecological reasons, it wasn't just one or two trees that decided to bloom in a year, it was all of them in the area.

The last nut year had been when Matsuri was only seven, but she still hadn't forgotten it. Even when the squirrel population boomed and they ate the lion's share of the nuts, the rejoicing of the villagers had gone on largely unabated. Matsuri had kept a sharp eye out whenever their orbiter passed over the island, looking for those specks of light color—the blooming flowers—among the deep green of the canopy.

When Matsuri's satchel was half full of nuts, she left the area.

The sun's still high. Maybe I'll go up the ridge a ways and look for some other fruit.

I might even find that durian.

She could practically taste the durian's sweet-and-sour milk already. If she had any trouble finding it, the bats and orangutan trails would point her in the right direction, and the effort would be worth it. Durian were few and far between. They weren't the only thing she was after, however. A nice jackfruit, or some figs, or the red fruit of the rambutan—any one of these would hit the spot. They were all delicious. Thoughts of culinary delights drifted through her head, and Matsuri's pace quickened.

Occasionally, she would stop and look up a tree. When she found a fruit, she shimmied up and plucked it. Whenever branch conditions dictated that she couldn't use both hands, she would knock the fruit off its branch and collect it from the ground. Several of them she ate on the spot.

Her bag was full, and Matsuri was about to head home when she detected something—a foreign smell in the jungle. She stopped.

Smells like...insect repellent.

Could it be someone from space? An anthropologist, perhaps? Someone in jungle development?

Matsuri's nose twitched and she followed the trail of the scent.

She had only walked a short while when she spotted something orange in the underbrush.

Matsuri strode over. "*Hoi?* Akane. What are you doing here?"

Akane lay listless, wedged between two large root-fins. Her face, hands, and clothes were covered in sweat and grime. She was lying on a silvery survival blanket.

The orange color came from the coveralls she was wearing—a standard-issue SSA uniform for flight crew. She had on a survival vest, which was covered with pockets large and small and held up by suspenders.

Akane slowly turned in the direction of the voice. "Matsuri?" A look of surprise came into her vacant eyes. When she sat up, it was with a frailty that made her seem three times her age.

"Want something to eat? They're yummy."

"Yes!" Akane's eyes went wide.

For the next ten seconds, she attacked Matsuri's stash with a vengeance. Then she looked up. "Thank you, but I really shouldn't be doing this. I'm not supposed to let anyone help me."

"*Hoi?* Why not?"

"I'm doing solo survival training—except it's more of a test than training."

"Oh." Matsuri nodded. Solo survival training was widely known as the most severe regimen used by the military—and by the SSA, as it happened. Personnel doing the training were given a limited amount of water, food, and gear and dropped off by helicopter in the middle of nowhere. Then they would have to navigate back to a designated place within a set amount of time, entirely on their own.

It was a test of decision-making ability, stamina, survival skills, and psychological resilience in the noisy solitude of the jungle. The training was famous in the military for higher-than-normal rates of attrition due to mental instability and in some cases, death.

Yukari had undergone solo survival training herself. In her case, it had gone rather smoothly after she met Matsuri on her first day in the jungle. With Matsuri's expert guidance, she'd had no trouble making it back home. As a test, it'd been a failure, but the SSA had already been committed to using Yukari before the test, and the addition of Matsuri to the team had been an added bonus.

"I had no idea you were even still on the island."

"It was supposed to be a secret. They were afraid that if you knew, one of you would try to help me. I camped overnight in the security forces' training area and trained for three days, then they brought me out here by helicopter."

"Wait, so how many days have you been in the jungle?"

"This is my third day. But if I don't make it home by midnight, I'll fail."

Akane lowered her eyes.

They had only given her a day's worth of food. She'd received general survival skills training for tropical and subtropical regions, but they hadn't taught her anything specific about the geography or edible flora of this particular island.

Akane had divided the food she was given into three portions, taking care not to eat too much on any day, but she was already at her limit with hunger. No matter how much she rested, once her strength failed it did not come back.

"We heard that you dropped out and went back to Japan."

"That's what they told you, huh."

"Yukari was very upset. She still is. She wanted to apologize to you."

"What? It was my choice to come here. Yukari has nothing to be sorry about!" Using the roots on either side as handholds, Akane staggered to her feet. She folded her blanket carefully and stashed it in her pack. Then she began to walk across the loamy soil, one step at a time.

"I have to get back...have to get back by midnight."

"*Hoi!* Well, if you want a shortcut—"

"No! Don't tell me!" Akane said sharply. "Don't help me. If you help me, I won't pass. Please."

Matsuri saw the look in Akane's eyes and fell silent. After a few moments she said, "You'll be fine, Akane. The weather's on your side today."

"Thanks. I'm going to give it one last shot."

Matsuri scanned their surroundings. Then she pointed up in the sky. "Look! Swallows! Ooh! Look at all of them!"

Akane followed the direction her fingers were pointing. Indeed, something was darting through the air beyond the dense foliage of the trees.

"Those are swallows?"

"Yep. They're awful good at flying, those swallows." Matsuri picked up her satchel and stood. "*Hoi!* I'm going to go gather some more fruit before I head back home." She walked off into the jungle, disappearing within moments, leaving Akane to ponder what she had said.

If she's going to gather more fruit, that means she's probably not headed straight back to base...

Akane was sure the other girl had been trying to tell her something indirectly, but what?

She looked back up at the wheeling swallows.

For some reason, it was a relief to see their familiar sweptback wing shape again. Swallows were common near her home in Japan. When they had first dropped her off in the jungle two days before, Akane had stared wide-eyed at everything, amazed by the rich abundance of life. Her joy hadn't lasted long.

Akane prided herself on having paid attention during biology class, but for whatever reason, she had never learned much about the tropics. *If I'd only studied more, I might know what around here is edible...*

Something brushed across the back corner of her mind. The wheeling swallows—swallows wheeled like that when they were catching insects to eat.

Which meant that there were insects up there. Probably a lot of them. Insects tended to swarm most immediately following eclosion—their emergence from a chrysalis, in other words.

Akane pricked up her ears. She could hear it now, a mass thrumming of wings. It was high-pitched. *Flies? No, bees.* They were most definitely small bees or wasps. She had read something about jungle wasps in a book about parasitic life-forms.

Akane wracked her brains for any shred of memory that might prove helpful.

Then it hit her: fig wasps!

Fig flowers bloomed internally—they were hard to see from the outside. For pollination, fig trees relied on wasps. Her biology teacher had called it a "masterpiece of symbiosis."

Fig flowers had male flowers, female flowers, and a third kind where wasps laid their eggs. Two wasps would actually mate inside the fruit, in contact with a male flower. Then, with the pollen still attached, the female wasp would fly off in search of an appropriate flower in which to lay her eggs. Since the female flower of the same plant was not shaped well for egg-laying, the wasp would look for a different tree, and pollination was accomplished.

How did I not realize this before now?

She had heard the humming of wasp wings several times already during the last two days and avoided them, fearing a sting. But she had never put two and two together to realize that where there were fig wasps, there were figs!

Akane walked closer to where the swallows danced in the sky. It didn't take her long to find a fig tree laden with fruit. She pulled off a fig and split it in half. It was perfectly ripe and full of juice. Akane crammed it in her mouth without even peeling off the skin, the sweet juice filling her mouth.

Her eyes watered with tears. She ate three of the figs, one right after the other. The fourth had a wasp inside it. After that, she was a little more careful in choosing her fruit. When she was satisfied, she stopped eating, afraid of a bellyache.

She picked off another ten good-looking figs and stashed them in her pack. The feeling of strength flowing back into her body was palpable. She checked her watch and found it was just after two o'clock.

I might just make it home. I've got another ten hours—four until sundown.

Matsuri must have walked from base, she reasoned. *And if she can do it, so can I.*

Then a troubling thought occurred to her. Had Matsuri helped her find the figs? All she had done was point out the swallows. It certainly hadn't seemed like a hint at the time. But Matsuri might've meant it as one. She had known that where there were swallows, there were figs.

But I was the one who put it all together.

She decided that if she made it back before the deadline, she would tell them what had happened. *Even if it disqualifies me, at least I'll be honest, and that has to count for something.*

Akane pulled out her compass and verified her course. She

didn't need a guide. Hints were everywhere if she just looked: the lay of the land, the vegetation, flocks of birds, flowing streams. She wouldn't miss another clue. Not this close to victory.

[ACT 10]

YUKARI WAS ON break, but she didn't much feel like doing anything, so instead of going out she lay on her bed in her room and read one of the books she'd bought in Yokohama. This one was titled *Zionism and Islamic Society*.

She heard the quick path of footsteps approaching and someone opened her door without knocking.

"*Hoi!* You won't believe how much fruit I nabbed, Yukari! Let's eat."

Yukari groaned and set her book down next to her pillow. "Just no durian, please."

"No problem! I've got nuts and rambutan and jackfruits and figs."

Yukari frowned. "Hey! No dirty sacks on my bed!"

Matsuri moved her satchel onto the floor and sat crosslegged on a chair. "What will it be?"

"A fig, I guess."

Matsuri handed her the fruit and Yukari began peeling it, a disinterested look on her face. Matsuri dug the flesh out of a rambutan with her army knife. The two ate their tropical meal in silence, tossing skins and seeds into a wastebasket and using tissues to wipe the juice from their lips. Only their hands and jaws moved.

Though Matsuri was customarily cheerful, she had never been a big talker. By comparison, Yukari hardly ever stopped talking, until now. She hadn't been much in the mood for conversation since Akane had left.

After several minutes of eating in silence, Matsuri wiped her mouth with the back of one hand and said, "So I met Akane in the jungle."

Yukari froze. "What did you say?"

"I said I met Akane in the jungle."

Yukari jumped from her chair. "You met Akane?" she shouted, fig seeds spraying from her lips. "In the jungle! Here?"

"Where else?" Matsuri asked.

"Why? How? Where?"

"I already told you. In the jungle. She was doing solo survival training. She's going to fail if she doesn't make it back before midnight tonight."

"Wait, but that means—" Yukari's eyes swam as her brain worked overtime to process the new information. "That means Akane hasn't failed! They lied to us!"

"Sounds like it. They probably lied so we wouldn't help her."

Yukari's face flushed with rage. *Why that weasel!* She dashed for the door, then stopped and whirled around. "Where was she, exactly? Was she far?"

"She was in the hills about three klicks from the eastern edge of the runway. She seemed pretty pooped."

Three kilometers was a long way in the jungle.

"She was tired? Well, what did you do? You helped her, right?"

"Nope. I left her there and went looking for more fruit."

"You didn't even show her the way back?"

"She asked me not to help her."

"Of all the—!"

Yukari stormed out of the room in a rage, ranting under her breath as she went. *I don't care why she did it. I'm going to give that woman a piece of my mind! I don't care if it was technically the right thing to do.*

Yukari ran, first to the women's dormitory in search of Satsuki Asahikawa, and when she wasn't to be found there, on to the training center. She ran up the stairs and knocked on the door to the lab.

The door was locked, but no one was inside.

Yukari checked around the center until she was sure no one was there.

"If she comes walking up tomorrow like nothing's happened—"

It was time for Plan B. She could go help her, but then again, Akane was one to play by the rules to a fault. Yukari wondered if there were any way she could lead Akane to the base without her even knowing it.

She checked her watch. It was five o'clock. Hardly any time left to do anything.

She would just have to wait and trust in Akane's ability. Even though she didn't trust it at all.

What if she's already here, just a little ways away? Yukari walked faster. The light outside was already an orange yellow. She made for the main gate, trailing a long shadow behind her. She told the guard she was just going out for a stroll and went through. Outside the base, Yukari stopped and held her breath. She was looking at the back of a white lab coat.

There you are.

Satsuki turned around, a look of surprise on her face. "Yukari? What are you doing outside at this time of day?"

"Just going for a little walk," Yukari replied, a bit too quickly.

Satsuki wouldn't know that her secret was out yet, and Yukari had nothing to gain by telling her. But what was *she* doing outside? Surely not waiting here for Akane's return?

"Here to meet someone, Satsuki?"

"You might say that."

"A guy?"

"Could be."

"You're not telling?"

"Do I have to?"

"No. Not really," Yukari said.

The conversation died on the spot. The two stood, about five meters apart, both standing facing toward the jungle.

It wasn't long before the sun brushed the ridgeline of the mountains to the west.

A hum rose from the forest as birds sang to one another, ascertaining the safety of their roosts. Far away, over the tops of the trees, Yukari saw something like a stream of black smoke.

"Bats," she said.

"That's what that is?" the doctor asked.

"They fly out of their caves in the evening like that. Matsuri told me."

"They don't attack people, do they?"

"Who knows?"

The last rays of light disappeared behind the tips of the trees.

"Yukari?"

"Yeah?"

"Look—"

"Yeah?"

They heard footsteps behind them. The two women turned. It was Kinoshita.

"Well, what do we have here?" he said bemusedly. He was dressed casually in a cotton shirt and loose-fitting slacks, but his hair was carefully combed back.

"Ooh! So you were waiting for Kinoshita?" Yukari teased.

Kinoshita and Satsuki exchanged quick glances.

"I'll leave that to your imagination," Kinoshita replied.

"I don't want to be a third wheel..."

"Not at all."

Kinoshita joined Satsuki by the big SOLOMON SPACE ASSOCIATION sign and the two stood there, showing no indications of going anywhere.

Because the sun set straight down in the tropics, it got dark very quickly. Yukari squinted, peering into the jungle, but she couldn't see any movement at all. Already an hour had passed since she came through the gate. Satsuki had made no attempt to restart their earlier conversation, and standing around in silence was growing pretty boring.

Frustratingly enough, her anger had entirely disappeared. She was still upset that no one had trusted her, but she wasn't entirely sure that she could have kept herself from interfering had she known. She could find absolutely no fault with them wanting Akane's final test to be a fair one. By now, they had probably realized she was onto them, anyway. Still, if the cover story was that Kinoshita and Satsuki were having a dalliance, she didn't want them to think she was being rude. Yukari was just about to say something when a fourth person came up behind them.

"*Hoi*, Yukari! Akane show up yet?"

With a few simple words, Matsuri turned the situation on its head.

Yukari looked up. Satsuki and Kinoshita were staring at the two of them in silence.

"Not yet."

"Well, she's still got six hours. She'll be fine."

"So you knew," Kinoshita said. It wasn't a question.

"Oh, I ran into her in the jungle today around lunchtime."

Kinoshita and Satsuki both turned to look at the guard by the gate, then back at Yukari.

"We were hoping to avoid that. Sorry we had to lie."

"It's okay. And Matsuri didn't help her," Yukari explained. "Akane told her not to."

"That so?"

"You don't have to believe me if you don't want to, but that's what she said."

"No, I believe you."

"Look, I see what you're doing, but isn't it a little abrupt to throw a girl fresh off the boat from Japan into a solo survival scenario?"

"We spent a whole week getting ready. And we've been far kinder than we would be to the usual applicants. There aren't any dangerous animals on the island, and she's carrying a transceiver. She'll have plenty of difficulties, but not so much danger."

"What about the poisonous snakes and poisonous frogs?"

"We took what preventative measures we could. We taught her how to inject herself with penicillin if it came to that," Satsuki said. "For what it's worth, this test wasn't my idea."

"It was mine," Kinoshita said. "Don't take it out on her."

"Whatever. It's fine." Yukari's shoulders slumped. She regretted not getting a chance to chew Satsuki out, but now she was too concerned for Akane's safety to worry much about that.

Kinoshita turned to Matsuri. "So, where was Akane when you found her?"

"About three klicks from the eastern edge of the runway."

"And when did you see her?"

"A little after noontime."

"I see. She's making good progress, then." Kinoshita walked over to the guardhouse and quickly returned.

A few moments later, a spotlight began sweeping across the sky. It came from behind the main complex and the training center—probably from the runway.

"Don't think I'm giving her any special treatment. This level of illumination is standard. Just don't ask me to set off the sirens."

Thanking him was the furthest thing from Yukari's mind, though she regretted not having thought of turning on the lights herself.

Together, the four of them waited.

A little after nine o'clock, Mukai and Nasuda joined them, having finished work.

When Mukai saw the crowd, he quickly went back, returning a few moments later with a large cooler in his arms.

"I brought some sandwiches and cola from the cafeteria."

Everyone held out their hands in silence. No one wanted to talk. It was hard not to feel guilty, standing there waiting for her.

Yukari turned to Matsuri. "So, jungle expert, what's the best possible route she could've taken?"

"Well, the easiest would have been to go straight north until she hit the ocean, then walk down the shore. That would get her out of the jungle more quickly."

"Right..."

That had been Yukari's plan when they sent her out. Once she reached the coast, she would just have to go east until she ran into the base, then follow the line of the fence to the front gate. Yukari turned to look down the fence, but it was lost in the darkness.

"Did she have a flashlight with her?"

"Yes, but batteries for only two hours. No spares," Kinoshita said. "Even if she saved them for her last day, they'd be dead by now."

"Any moon tonight?"

"Not until the early morning," Matsuri said.

"You could have at least waited until a full moon!" Yukari growled.

"Now now, Yukari." Nasuda had just begun to console her when Matsuri waved for them to be silent. "*Hoi?* I saw something flash."

"Where?"

Everyone turned to look in the direction Matsuri was pointing.

For a while they saw nothing. But then, several minutes later, all six of them gasped. Off in the jungle, a light twinkled. From the position, it was about half a kilometer away, moving down a slope.

"Where is she, Matsuri?"

"I think she was moving to the left. So she's going for the main road, not the coast."

"Think she'll make it?"

"She's about to head into a small valley. If she cuts straight across it, she'll be fine, but if she tries to walk along it she'll get into trouble."

"What kind of trouble?"

"Swamp trouble."

Yukari swallowed. Just because they had spotted her didn't mean she was going to make it. She kept watching the jungle, but the light was nowhere to be seen. Yukari had never considered herself to be particularly religious, but now she was praying with all her might.

She glanced at her watch. Eleven o'clock.

"There it is again!"

They spotted the light, this time much farther to the left than before.

"She's past the valley."

"Really?"

"As long as she keeps walking straight, she'll make it to the road."

"Thatta girl!" Yukari cupped her hands around her mouth like a megaphone and took a deep breath.

"Don't," Kinoshita said quickly. "This is a test. She has to make it to the very end on her own."

Yukari blew out her lungful of air quietly and squinted into the darkness. The road went straight into the jungle before it curved. From just around the curve, she could see a yellow light flickering.

"She made it, Yukari. She's on the road."

Finally, they saw her emerge from between the trees. She was wobbling slightly, a makeshift torch in her right hand.

Yukari could restrain herself no longer. "Akane! Hey! Over here!"

Akane waved her torch in response.

"You did it!" Yukari shouted again, doing a little dance. "You did it, Akane!"

Now she could see the other girl's orange coveralls. Akane's feet dragged as she walked, but her progress was steady. Yukari ran up to the edge of where the paved road from the base ended and waited there like a relay runner waiting for her turn with the baton.

When she got closer, Akane threw her torch down on the ground and practically collapsed into Yukari's arms. Yukari patted her cheek, covered with scrapes and mud.

"You did it, Akane. You really did it."

Steadying her shoulders, she helped Akane sit down. Beside them, Satsuki knelt and began a cursory examination.

"Any injuries?"

"No...I'm fine."

"How do you feel?"

"Good. No, great."

"You did a great job."

"The torch was a good idea," Kinoshita said.

"I found some resinous branches on the fig tree and gathered them before it got too dark."

"Well," Nasuda said, extending his hand, "I think we've got our third astronaut."

Akane reached out to shake his hand, then suddenly jerked away. "I..." she began, "I met Matsuri in the jungle." Akane explained what had happened and how she had found the fig trees.

"Matsuri?" Nasuda turned to her. "What were you really up to out there? Did you mean to give her that hint?"

Matsuri shook her head. "Oh, I don't think about those difficult kinds of things. I just thought the swallows were really cool. I wanted Akane to see them too."

"Hmm. What do you think, Satsuki?"

"I think that Matsuri could tell me she'd ridden a pink elephant and I'd believe her." Satsuki chuckled.

"Well then, there you have it." Nasuda turned to Akane. "Congratulations, you passed."

"Th-thank you, sir!"

"Training starts tomorrow," Satsuki joined in. "If you've got what it takes to make it out there, I'm sure you can take a few extra G. Eight, maybe?"

"Well, I..."

"You'll do your best," Satsuki said with a wink.

The training center gym, one week later.

While the gym wasn't strictly off-limits to men, they had to be careful when visiting. The gym was where the astronauts let it all hang out. Right now Yukari and Matsuri were in their space suits. The door opened. "Here she is!" a voice announced.

It was chief chemical engineer Motoko Mihara, leading Akane behind her in a brand-new formfitting space suit.

While Akane lacked the curves of the other two girls, she was very trim and the supporting nature of the suit's fabric made her look great.

"Hey hey hey! Not bad!"

"You look great, Akane."

"You'll have your share of fans in no time, Akane!"

"What? Fans?" Akane's face turned bright red and she held her hands over her chest and stomach.

"Don't hide yourself like that," Yukari said. "It just makes you look like you're being coy. You gotta walk like you mean it. You'll get used to it soon."

"But it's like...it's like I'm naked," Akane said quietly.

Motoko chuckled behind her thick-rimmed glasses. "If so then I did my job right. It's supposed to fit like a second skin, you know."

The space suits were Motoko's pet project. With each revision the fabric and fittings felt better and better. Though they were easiest to wear while seated in the cockpit, their flexibility made them perfectly comfortable while standing and walking also.

There was a knock at the door. "Can I come in?" It was Nasuda.

He was wearing a suit. He stared at Akane for a moment then clapped his hands together. "All right, definitely astronaut material!"

"Please..." Akane said, mortified.

"Stop covering yourself up like that, it makes it worse," Yukari said.

"Not that they will in that suit, but if anyone ever doubts you're an astronaut, you'll always have this," Nasuda said, offering a small booklet to Akane. "It's your astronaut's passport."

Inside the booklet was a laminated picture of her face, next to text reading ASTRONAUT AKANE MIURA. On the next page a message had been written in ten languages. Japanese was at the top. "The bearer of this document has been recognized by Japan and the Solomon Islands as an astronaut, and the Solomon Space Association hereby requests all whom it may concern to allow the bearer to pass freely and without hindrance and to afford the bearer all necessary assistance and protection."

"Hold on to this, and no matter where in the world you land, your human rights will be protected."

"Wow, astronauts really are like citizens of the world."

"It only helps if you happen to land where there are people, of course."

Yukari shook her head. "I'll take the open sea to the Nellis Academy gardening club's fishpond any day."

CHAPTER THREE

OPERATION: RESCUE ORPHEUS

[ACT 1]

"SAY AGAIN, HOUSTON? I didn't copy." Norman Randolph had heard Houston loud and clear. He just didn't like what they were telling him.

"We're showing a problem with one of Orpheus's attitude control thrusters. Two sensors are coming up red."

"You expect me to fix that up here? We're not exactly packing spare parts for the probe."

"We can't deploy until we get this cleared up."

"Roger that, Houston," Norman grumbled into the comm. This was one fight he wouldn't be winning. "What am I in for?"

In a NASA-issue space suit, no one can see you shrug. This was the last thing he wanted to be doing right now, but if he made too much of a fuss, he might lose his chance to ever launch again.

It had taken five years for him to make it on a flight after he had been added to the space shuttle crew. The average lifetime total flights for a NASA astronaut was a paltry three. If you didn't want that to be a hard limit, you had to be very patient and pick your battles.

"I'm moving you, Norman. You ready?"

That was Gordon Krenic, radioing him from the cabin. Norman's feet were fixed to the tip of the Remote Manipulation Arm that unfolded like an insect leg from the shuttle's cargo bay. Gordon controlled the arm from inside the cabin.

"Go for it."

The arm lifted Norman's body three meters upward where it stopped with a light quiver from the inertia. He was farther away from the floor of the payload bay now, able to see both wings of the shuttle and beyond that, the blue arc of the earth.

The unmanned probe known as Orpheus was right in front of him. The upper-stage engine that would send the probe all the way to Pluto was positioned on the underside relative to his position. Together, the probe and engine extended from the center of the payload bay, like a giant cannon pointing toward space. The scale was impressive.

Norman knew that this large-scale probe would most likely be the last of its kind.

With each passing year, the probes had been getting smaller and smaller, lifted into space by small, unmanned rockets. Using the shuttle to bring the probe into low orbit, manually extending all the antennas, and doing a careful systems check all took too much time and manpower—these costs would kill such projects.

The Orpheus Project had started back when people still viewed the shuttle through rose-colored glasses. It was only a short while after the shuttle began operation that its lack of cost-effectiveness really came to the surface, but it was the explosion of the *Challenger* in '86 that changed everything. The flight schedule was cut in half, and safety became a top priority. The Orpheus Project was put on ice for years.

With guidance from Houston, Norman began the task of removing the gold-colored thermal blanket covering the surface of the probe. On the ground, this would have been no more difficult than ripping open an envelope, but up here it was next to impossible. He had to exert a pressure of at least thirty kilograms just to grab something with his stiff space suit gloves, and he could feel absolutely nothing through the thick fabric. That, and the arm he was standing on wobbled like a fishing pole.

Finally he got the blanket off, revealing the duralumin structure beneath.

Norman fished an Allen wrench out of his pocket and set about tightening the screws, keeping his left hand hovering over them so he wouldn't lose anything to space.

Removing the eight screws took all of forty minutes.

Once the panel was open, he could see tubes for hydrogen underneath. Next to them was the control valve assembly. In all, it was about the size of a portable radio. Norman took one look at the nest of wires and tubing connected to the control valve and sighed. *They want me to remove that?*

"Ever build a ship in a bottle?" he muttered to no one in particular. "That's what this feels like."

"Pull it off, and you'll be a hero," said a voice over his radio from inside the shuttle. This was the captain, Wayne Berkheimer.

It was true. Fixing a problem while in orbit was an astronaut's chance to shine. When people back home heard the news, it reminded them of the need for manned missions.

It took Norman three hours to remove the valve assembly. With his left hand, he hugged it tightly to his chest. Now all he needed to do was bring it back inside the shuttle where they could take a close look at it.

"It's done," Norman said, relieved. "Bring me back to the air lock, Gordon."

"Well," Gordon said over the radio, "you'll be coming back up here again for sure."

The remote manipulating arm began to move.

"Wait!" Norman barked, "not that way!"

He could hear Gordon swearing under his breath over the radio. The arm holding Norman in place was about to collide with one of the antennas protruding from the probe. The inertia of the arm was such that it was hard to stop quickly. Norman ducked, hoping to avoid the antenna entirely. It took all of his strength to move in his bulky suit, and in his rush, he forgot to pay attention to what he was holding in his left hand.

As the antenna swooshed soundlessly over his head, the valve assembly drifted from his fingers, spinning through space toward the probe's engine.

The valve hit one of the exterior panels and ricocheted off into a gap between the main body of the probe and the engine.

"Dammit!"

"Sorry about that, Norman. You okay?"

"I'm fine, but I lost the valve assembly. I think it's lodged inside the connector between the probe and the engine."

"Roger that. What do you want me to do?"

"Bring me a little closer to the probe again. About three feet."

"Okay. I'll try not to mess this one up."

Once he was close enough, Norman peered at the connector. The connector was like a deep, wedge-shaped groove in the side of the probe, fifty centimeters wide and about three meters in diameter. The engine was designed to detach once the probe was on its interplanetary trajectory. There was a ring of shaped explosives for this purpose connected to the probe by a complex truss, making the area around the connector look like a jungle gym.

Norman shone in his light and spotted the valve assembly wedged inside the crevice.

"Found it...I think I might be able to reach." Norman stuck his hand down into the groove but was unable to reach it. In the space suit, his arm was about three times bulkier than it was in normal clothes, and he couldn't get his joints to bend around the frame.

When he finally did reach the valve assembly, he only succeeded in brushing it with the tips of his fingers, which knocked it farther into the wedge—a fatal mistake.

"Godamnit! Now it's wedged in next to the tank!"

"Think you'll be able to get it out soon?" the captain asked.

"No, definitely not soon. Maybe not at all."

"Right. Then come back to the shuttle for now. I'm sure we'll think of some other way to go after it."

[ACT 2]

"TURN THE VOLUME up! Louder!" someone shouted on the other side of the cafeteria.

Yukari, Matsuri, and Akane put down their lunches and looked up. Every eye in the cafeteria was glued to the large television screen on the wall. Someone had changed the channel from the usual Japanese broadcast to CNN.

"Wonder what it is? Maybe they're showing something about us?"

"*Hoi!* Let's go check it out."

The three stood and walked over closer to the screen.

They were showing a live feed, apparently from the space shuttle. The picture was being taken from the rear observation window on the upper deck, showing two astronauts in the middle of the payload bay, working on some device.

Someone turned the volume up and they could hear an anchorwoman's voice, saying, "*...into the third day. The part seems to have gotten wedged inside a crevice in the Orpheus probe too deep to be easily* *removed. They've tried shaking it and using a gripping extension hand, but so far they've had no luck in retrieving the wayward part."*

"Yikes! They're still working on that thing?" Yukari said. A man in coveralls in front of her turned.

"They just might need you up there, Yukari."

"Nah!"

"You never know."

"Apparently, it will be impossible to retrieve the part without dismantling the engine array on the probe, and this will be impossible to do while in orbit."

"The director is already moving on this," the man said. "They've got a booster under assembly in the VAB. Just making preparations at this point, but still."

"You mean the SSA is going to go up there?" Akane asked.

"Why not?" the man asked. "One of you could slide your whole body in there and fish it out, no problem."

Akane returned her gaze to the television. "I don't know. It looks pretty tight."

For the last month, Akane had been training in the training center's pool.

She would get into her space suit, strap on a backpack, and attach the appropriate amount of ballast to make the experience of floating in water as close to being weightless as possible. While submerged, they had her putting together mock-up satellites and taking them apart.

"The shuttle will only be up for another three days. NASA has said they will do everything they can while there's still time remaining. However, in the worst-case scenario, they'll be obligated to bring the Orpheus probe back down to the ground with them."

"That'll be the end of that project," the man in the overalls said.

"Couldn't they just fix it and relaunch?" Akane asked.

The man shook his head. "Hardly. The shuttle schedule is booked solid for the next ten years. That probe was sitting in a warehouse for ten years before it even got to go up the first time. There's no guarantee it'll be serviceable when its time comes around again."

"That sounds like a waste."

"Sounds like business as usual in space development to me. Me, I work on support booster shielding. It takes about four months to finish those. Four months to make, and they throw them away after two minutes into launch."

"I had no idea," Akane said, looking down.

"Hey, I don't mind," the man said. "At least they serve their purpose. Those one-shot-only modules can't be fully tested, so you really have to know your stuff in order to make them. Not that you should worry. I know my stuff."

One of the man's friends came by and told him to stop bragging.

Akane nodded, thinking to herself.

The girls met back at their seats and resumed lunch. Yukari was eating a whitefish meuniere, Matsuri an omelette, and Akane had chosen a marinated octopus dish. For starch, each of them had rice. Though there were some local islanders on staff, the majority of people in the cafeteria were Japanese, and the food was hardly different from what they got back home.

"You eat like a bird, Akane. Don't you get hungry?" Yukari asked.

"Well, to tell the truth I would like a little more, but I only have three hours until you know what..."

"Oh, right."

"You-know-what" was centrifuge training. Akane's studies and operational training were both going perfectly smoothly. The only hiccup: lack of high-G resilience.

"How's that going? Getting used to it?"

"Not really. I can only last five seconds or so at 8 G."

"Five seconds? That's plenty. That's all you have to take during the real thing."

"But on a real liftoff you have vibration too, so Satsuki says I need extra tolerance to get through—"

"You do get rattled around a fair bit."

"That, and the high G on reentry lasts a lot longer." Akane sighed.

"Don't worry so much. You've got another five months before your first flight. You'll get used to it in time."

"Just sleep on it tonight. I'll get you up!" Matsuri said cheerfully.

Yukari rolled her eyes. "That's very nice of you, Matsuri, but do you mind wiping your mouth with a napkin or something? You're covered in ketchup."

"Oh, I'll get it later."

"No, wipe right when it gets on you. That's called being civilized."

"Civilized people sure have it tough."

"Yes, we like it that way."

"*Hoi.*"

"That reminds me," Akane said suddenly. "You say *hoi* a lot, Matsuri, but what does it mean?"

"It doesn't mean anything at all," Yukari declared.

"Really?" Akane asked.

"Either that or it means everything."

Akane looked confused.

"You explain it, Matsuri!"

"*Hoi?*"

"Do you have any idea what we're talking about?"

"*Hoi.*"

"There. See what she did?" Yukari fumed. "That's the way it always is with her. That's the way it is with everyone down here in the South Pacific. You don't have to have a sensible conversation because you don't need to actually communicate information to survive. All you need are a few coconut trees and you're golden."

Akane shook her head and chuckled. She was about to tear apart Yukari's theory when a blaring announcement from the PA system cut her off.

"All astronauts to the briefing room immediately. I repeat, all astronauts to the briefing room immediately."

[ACT 3]

THEY ARRIVED AT the briefing room to find Nasuda, Kinoshi-ta, and Satsuki already there, waiting for them. When they were seated at the round table, Nasuda spoke.

"Sorry for the last-minute nature of this, but we've been called upon to participate in an emergency mission. We're launching to-morrow at 10:34 AM sharp. We'll be using the orbiter *Mangosteen*. Yukari will be captain, and Akane will be MS. Matsuri, you'll be backup here with the ground crew."

The room was silent.

"You said mission specialist Akane?" Akane said in a voice that was barely a whisper.

"That's right."

Her mouth hung open. "You mean I'm going up? Already?"

Nasuda nodded deeply. "That's correct. I know it's a lot earlier than we had originally scheduled, but, well, congratulations."

"But why—"

"Allow me to explain the mission first."

"Is this about the Orpheus?" Yukari asked.

"That's correct. We're going to help them launch that unlucky Pluto-bound probe. They're flying in a replacement for the part that got damaged to us now. It should get here tomorrow morn-ing. You'll bring the part up to the shuttle and retrieve the bro-ken part that's gotten wedged inside the probe engine block. That's your mission." Nasuda stared at each of the girls in turn. "We're going to fix NASA's mistake and show them how good we are at extravehicular activity. I hardly need to say that this is our big chance."

"And we'll get to show off our new recruit to NASA at the same time."

"Exactly. I want them to know that we have an MS at the SSA too. Akane, you'll be performing the EVA to retrieve the jammed part."

"But I can't do that!" Akane practically shouted. "I was supposed to train for six months! I've only had one!"

"The training program is intended to prepare you for solo flight. You'll have Yukari with you."

"I'll just get in the way!"

Nasuda frowned. He knew it was a bold move to go with the new recruit, but he wasn't ready to give up on this one just yet.

Yukari glanced at Satsuki. *She must've been against this. Her face says it all.*

"Well, I don't want to create trouble before we've even launched," Nasuda said. "I'll take your feelings under advisement. If you don't feel you're ready to fly, I'll swap you out for Matsuri. How do you feel about that, Yukari?"

Yukari could sense Akane's worried gaze on her.

"You think Akane isn't up to the job?" Nasuda asked again.

"She is," Yukari said crisply. "No problem."

"Yu-Yukari!" Akane stammered. Yukari cut her off.

"I *said* no problem. You'll be fine."

"But I can't go into space tomorrow, I'm not—"

"You can! I'll be with you!"

"But..."

"Don't you want to go to space?"

"Well, yes, but—"

"Then you can't pass up a single chance. The SSA won't be here forever. Blink and it might blow away. If we have even one major accident the whole thing's getting shut down. That's why if you get a chance to go, you better take it."

Akane's eyes rolled up into her head as she let Yukari's words sink in.

Yukari could be just as pushy as Nasuda in her own way.

One look at Akane was enough to tell how fast the girl's mind was racing. She sat there, thinking it over for a full sixteen seconds. "I'll go," she said at last.

"All right!" Yukari and Nasuda said at the same time.

That's a load off my shoulders, Yukari thought. *Fly just this once, Akane. Fly, and then you get to choose what comes next.*

"I'm amazed NASA came to you with this," Yukari said to Director Nasuda. "They wouldn't even let us get near their precious station."

"Who said anything about them coming to us? We went to them. And we gave them insanely good terms. They only pay up if we're successful."

Yukari sighed. "I should have guessed." Not that it was a surprise to anyone by this point, but it was becoming increasingly clear just how much of the SSA was run by this one man's ambition.

"So we're going up there without any specific training, then?"

"No, you'll train. Starting right now," Kinoshita said.

"How? We going to take the Gulfstream to Houston and get back in time for lunch?"

"That would be ideal, but we haven't got that kind of time. We're going to use a CG simulation to give you an idea of the conditions you will probably be facing up there."

"What?" Yukari said. "Computer graphics?"

"Think of it as a puzzle game. We've got all the data we need from NASA. You've got to get a good night's sleep tonight, so you'd better start training now."

[ACT 4]

THE SPACE SHUTTLE *Atlantis* was high in the sky over the Indian Ocean, getting ready for its fifty-seventh night since launch. By the ship clock it was noon. The shuttle crew had gathered in the middeck for lunch.

They were injecting hot water into bags of freeze-dried soup, which they then drank through straws, squeezing the bags to get out every last drop. The mood was sour. They were used to space food by now, but after four days of fruitless effort, who could blame them for wanting a real meal.

"So these girls are really coming tomorrow?" Norman asked. "Doesn't it usually take a whole day just to orchestrate a rendezvous?"

"We're going to do an immediate transfer after they've made their first orbit," the captain replied calmly. He was an ex-test pilot, and there was very little that ever ruffled his feathers. "I don't know what magic tricks they're using, but their orbital entry paths are frighteningly precise."

"So they come up here and then wriggle around inside that probe?"

"I'll believe it when I see it," pilot Luis Kreeger said. "I saw them on TV and I'm pretty sure they were using special effects. I mean, come on, a sixteen-year-old girl? What is this, some kind of anime?"

"What's 'anime'?"

"Japanese animation. There's always these little girls doing stuff. I'll loan you a tape when we get back."

"Well, we'd best get ready all the same," the captain said.

"Get ready for what?"

"Get ready for what will happen if these 'little girls' pull it off."

The crew exchanged glances. They were all men, and all winners in that desperate race to get to space. None of them were accustomed to losing, ever.

After a long while, Norman said, "I'm fine with that. Better than everything falling through and then having to go face Dr. O'Reilly." No one said anything, so Norman continued. "You know, he wouldn't blame us either. 'You did well, Norm. You'll get another chance.'"

Norman squeezed the last drops out of his bag of chicken soup and pushed it into the trash dispenser with a loud *thunk*.

"Dammit," Norman spat. "I don't want another chance. I want this one!"

[ACT 5]

SATSUKI'S MORNING CALL woke the three astronauts up the next morning at five o'clock sharp.

After Akane had been formally accepted by the association, she had moved into the dormitory on base together with the other two girls. They were each given their own private room on the second floor, with Yukari's room in the corner, then Matsuri's, then Akane's.

"*Hoi!* Yukari! Wakey-wakey!" Matsuri shouted from the hallway outside Yukari's door. Matsuri was always the first one to get up, so it was her job to make sure the other two weren't still snoozing.

When Yukari finally walked out into the hall, she found Akane there as well.

"Morning. You get any sleep, Akane?"

"Strangely enough, I slept like a baby."

"Wow. I always took you for the jittery type."

"I think I was probably pretty exhausted."

Yukari had gone right to sleep after the training ended, but even still it meant she had only gotten four hours. It was nowhere near enough. They left the dormitory and made for the cafeteria, squinting their eyes against the morning sun.

"Oh, now I get why it's so quiet," Yukari said. "No press."

The mission had been decided so suddenly there hadn't been any time for the press to get down to the island.

"Is there usually quite a lot?"

"Usually we can't even go eat breakfast before they make us hold a little press conference right here in front of the dormitory."

"They'll probably be landing pretty soon. The director loves his publicity," Matsuri said.

They went into the cafeteria and sat down at the counter without picking up trays.

"I'll take the special," Yukari said, waving to one of the cooks.

"Coming right up."

The clerk handed her a tray with toast, an egg, and coconut milk. It was a specially prepared, completely hygienic meal for astronauts. Yukari normally would have liked a little more to eat, but overeating before a launch was never a good idea.

"Good luck up there," Bishop said.

"Thanks."

"And good luck on your first flight, Akane."

Akane beamed. "Thank you!"

After they had eaten, the three of them went down for an examination at the training center. Satsuki took their temperatures, blood pressure, heart rate, and urine samples. She was moving fast, recording everything methodically in her notebooks.

"That's a clean bill of health for all three of you. You can go down to the control center now, Matsuri. You other two stay."

Satsuki made a phone call to the director's office. "Yukari and Akane are both good to go."

The next part was the worst. Satsuki had to give both girls an enema, injecting cold water from below to clean out their large intestines. This saved them from having to do a "number two" anytime soon.

Then they put on the space suits and did their hair.

"You and Matsuri have such long hair—doesn't it get in the way?" Akane asked.

"Actually," Yukari told her, "it makes it easier to wrap up that way."

Yukari split her hair into two braids, fixed them with hairbands, and applied a little hairspray. "Not that short hair is bad, either. As long as it doesn't get tangled in the adapter ring, it's fine."

"I see."

"Let's take a look at you!" Yukari turned to the other girl, helped her straighten her hair, and cut a few stray strands. "I love your hair, Akane. It's so light. Not heavy and matted like mine."

"I usually don't put anything in it at all."

"Well, if you don't now, you'll look like the Bride of Frankenstein when we get up there. Close your eyes." Yukari carefully applied hairspray to Akane's hair.

Then both of the girls put on their helmets, checked the seals, and they were ready. They were just about to walk out of the room when Akane stopped. "Um, actually, can you wait just one moment?"

"Sure."

Akane quickly called home. Her parents already knew about the flight, but she hadn't been able to talk to them herself, she'd been so busy since the night before.

"Miura speaking."

It was her brother, four years younger than she.

"Hideto? It's me."

"Akane! Your timing sucks."

"Huh?"

"Mom and Dad just went to the shrine. They're going to pray for you."

"Oh...right."

"Are you going to be on TV? It's your first flight, right?"

"No. The press won't make it here in time."

"Well, I'm pretty sure Mom and Dad'll be back soon. Can you call again?"

"I don't think so. I'm heading out to the launch pad right now. Can you just tell them that I'll call when I'm back?"

"Sure thing."

"All right, thanks, Hideto. School going okay?"

"You know me. I got the right stuff. Oh wait, no, that was you." Akane laughed. "Okay, well I'm going."

"Yup! Catch you la—"

She set down the receiver and quickly left the room.

Satsuki led the two astronauts down to the front of the training center, where both a cameraman from public relations and Nasuda waited. Nasuda squinted at them, sizing them up.

"Yukari, you're in charge of taking stock of the situation and making the calls up there. I want you to show them how we work."

"I'm on it."

"Akane. I know this is sudden, and you probably have some reservations, but I wouldn't ask you to do this if I didn't think you could handle it. This is your first flight. Have fun."

"Will do!"

"Right." Nasuda's eyes twinkled behind his glasses. "Now go show NASA what we're made of."

Yukari smiled, getting into the spirit of things for the first time.

Satsuki, Yukari, and Akane piled into the security vehicle and took off for the launch pad. They could see their destination for the entire journey down the two-kilometer stretch of road. The pad stood forty meters high, including the weather observatory station on top. The rocket, primed with liquid oxygen, was giving off white steam.

It was twenty-seven meters from the base to the tip of the rocket. Twenty meters of that was the LS-6 main booster. Two smaller solid-fuel boosters, used to get the rocket off the ground, were attached to either side of the main. If a rocket applied only as much force as it weighed, then it would just spend fuel without going anywhere. The solid boosters were there to push the rocket quickly up to the point where the atmosphere thinned out. Once the solid boosters separated, the main booster took over. The main booster burn was long and controlled, aiming more for conservation of velocity than brute thrust.

At that point, the crew would already be sixty kilometers up and flying nearly parallel to the ground, with very little air resistance, meaning they required little thrust to keep going. The most important thing was to use a minimum amount of fuel in the most efficient way possible to continue climbing.

The booster was aided in this by the fact that as it used fuel, the booster got lighter, adding to its acceleration. By the time they were out of fuel, they would be pushing back into their seats under 8 G of pressure—the fastest point in the launch sequence. That moment would be Akane's first real test.

They got out of the Humvee off to one side of the launch pad. There they stood for a moment, looking up at the rocket towering over them. The three of them got into the elevator. The air had been perfectly calm at ground level, but twenty meters up, there was a light breeze. A thin walkway extended from the elevator door to the orbiter.

"How do you feel?" Satsuki asked.

"Right as rain."

"I'm fine."

"Okay then. Good luck."

"Thanks."

"Here goes!"

Together, Yukari and Akane crossed the boarding bridge. They opened the orbiter hatch and sat down inside, bodies facing upward toward the sky, Yukari on the left and Akane on the right. The seats had been molded to each of their bodies, making for perfect fits.

They attached cables to the connectors on their space suits and fastened eight-point harnesses to their shoulders, chests, waists, and knees. Now the only things they could move were their heads and arms.

Yukari scanned the control panel, reviewed all of the key switches, then flipped the master power switch.

Air conditioning on. Cabin lights on.

When the hatch closed, cutting off their view of the outside, it was like they had taken their first step into space. The two girls' eyes met.

"This is it."

"Yep."

Her voice was quiet, but Yukari could tell that Akane was ready to go. The other girl took a deep breath, set her jaw, and turned her gaze to the instrument panel.

"Whew, it's the same," she whispered. Then more loudly, "It's all the same as in the procedure simulation."

"Yep. The acceleration feels just like the centrifuge, the view's the same, and all the communications are the same. If you want to know what's different—"

"I'll find out when we start moving?"

"That's right. Gives you something to look forward to."

Yukari flipped on the communicator switch. "Solomon Mission Control? This is *Mangosteen*. You read me?"

"*Hoi*, Yukari! Loud and clear!" Matsuri's voice came over their speakers. Contact with base was, as a rule, handled by the backup astronaut. Since they went through the same training they knew best how the other astronauts thought, which made communication easier.

As flamboyant as she could sometimes be, Matsuri did her job well, and Yukari had great faith in her. She had to be exceptionally intelligent as well, considering that she went from living among her tribe to manning a solo space flight in the space of three months.

The event clock showed T minus one hour fifty-four minutes.

Ballpoint pen in hand, Yukari began to read off her prelaunch checklist.

"One, pyrotechnics safety switch."

Akane checked and responded, "Locked."

"Two, attitude control handle."

"Locked."

"Three, abort handle."

"Locked."

And so on down the list. It was rumored that the entire purpose of the checklist was to keep the astronauts from getting bored, but Yukari always made sure to follow it to the letter.

It was always better to check for yourself instead of trusting someone else. Though the number of things one could check inside the cockpit was limited, if you did all you could, then you could at least sign off on that portion of the checklist. After that, you waited for fate to decide—at least that was how Yukari liked to think about it. It helped control the fear.

Even though this was Yukari's fifth launch, she still felt that familiar fear gnawing at her stomach. Just three meters beneath them were explosives equal in power to a tactical nuke, enough to accelerate them up to Mach 26 in the space of several minutes. Two girls who couldn't even legally drive scooters would be accelerating faster than a military fighter pilot. Of course it was frightening.

Yukari occasionally looked up to check on how Akane was doing. The other girl was marking off each item as she read aloud carefully.

Thatta girl.

Of course, in a sense, Akane had it easy. Every SSA rocket previous to Yukari's first flight had exploded moments after launch.

T minus thirty-five minutes. A large clanging sound rang from outside the orbiter. Akane sat up straight in her seat, pricking up her ears. "What was that?"

"The movable tower just disengaged. It means we're on schedule."

"Oh, right. It caught me off-guard."

"That's one thing the simulator lacks: the sounds." Yukari began to explain all the noises Akane would hear while on the ship. "The high-pitched buzzing sound is the electrical inverter. The light sloshing sound is the liquid oxygen tank. The low temperature system makes a *dong* sound every once in a while, but that's normal too. And the sound from the ventilation is just a fan."

Akane nodded, taking it all in.

"Just before we take off they'll repressurize the liquid oxygen tank. The noise is a little shocking. Sounds like things ripping apart, so get ready for it."

"You're very observant, aren't you, Yukari," Akane said, looking up at the other girl with respect in her eyes.

"That has nothing to do with it. You'll hear everything yourself whether you want to or not."

T minus fifteen minutes.

The countdown was proceeding apace. Pretty soon that ripping sound Yukari had warned Akane about filled the cabin.

"LOX tank, pressure normal."

"All systems are looking good, Yukari. How are you doing, Akane?"

"I'm doing great, Matsuri. A little excited, maybe."

"That's the way to be! Keep a bright heart, and the evil spirits won't want to have anything to do with you."

"I'll remember that, thanks."

T minus five minutes. In five minutes, they'd be shooting into space. Nearly every device in the cockpit was active and whirring now, the various sounds blending into one steady hum. The two girls lowered the airtight visors on their helmets and talked over their intercoms. The time for chitchat was over.

"Flight control data, check."

"Control data, check."

"Clock operation, check."

"Clock is functional."

"APU standby switch, on."

"APU standby switch, on."

T minus three minutes.

"Access arm stowed. Begin filling launch pad—intercom volume, plus two."

"Intercom volume, plus two."

This was to prepare for the roar of liftoff. They could hear water splashing like a waterfall down onto the launchpad.

"Looks like we're really going. Usually if we make it this far, we're set," Yukari explained.

Akane only nodded in reply.

"Oxygen release valve closed. Liftoff pressure."

"*Mangosteen*, all systems are functional."

T minus sixty seconds.

"Switch to internal electrical power. Orbiter voltage, check."

"Voltage is normal."

T minus twenty seconds.

"Solid boosters, APU start."

"APU start. I can hear them."

T minus fourteen seconds.

"All systems go! Get ready!"

"Yukari, Akane, we have a green light for takeoff. T minus ten, nine, eight, seven—main booster ignition—four, three, two—solid boosters ignition."

The entire orbiter shook as the shock wave from the solid boosters made the craft vibrate like a drum. The anchoring bolts on the launch pad flew off, and the rocket was free.

Akane felt her body sink into her chair.

"Launch site clear—*Mangosteen* is airborne," Matsuri announced as though she were giving the weather.

Yukari made her first report. "This is *Mangosteen*. We're climbing steadily. Akane, we're on our way."

"Uh-huh," Akane managed in a hoarse whisper.

Outside their window was only sky.

Their speed climbed violently. With only a tenth of the space shuttle's weight, SSA rockets took off like ballistic missiles.

Inside the cockpit, the vibrations grew steadily worse. Though from space the earth's atmosphere looked paper-thin, this was where rockets had to pass their first hurdle—the struggle against air resistance. Just before and after the point of maximum dynamic pressure—the point called "max Q"—the rocket shook like it was being pelted with hail. That came around T plus sixty seconds, at an altitude just below ten thousand meters.

"Yukari, Akane? Get ready for max Q."

"A-all systems operational," Yukari said through clenched teeth. "You h-hanging in there, Akane?"

"Y-yeah."

"The G's pretty bad but the sh-shaking's going to stop soon."

"O-okay."

After about a minute, the vibrations died down.

"Through max Q. All systems operational."

"Great stuff!"

Don't jinx us, Yukari thought. She checked the altimeter. They were already over thirty kilometers up, flying at an angle of forty-five degrees with their heads pointing toward the ground. You didn't feel like you were upside down, though. You just saw the earth above you.

"You can see the ocean out the window now."

"Hey, you're right. It's so blue."

"Still hanging in there?"

"So far."

T plus 140 seconds. They were at an altitude of sixty-eight kilometers now. With a ringing thud, the solid boosters separated and fell away.

"SRB separation lamps on."

"Hnnk." Akane grunted. The Gs climbed rapidly immediately after the solid boosters dropped.

Matsuri's voice came over the transceiver again. "Solid booster separation went great."

Stop saying that, you'll jinx us!

"Akane, this next part is the toughest."

She must have heard her grunt over the radio.

"I-I know," Akane managed to squeeze out the words. Her chest was rising and falling rapidly.

"Matsuri," Yukari cut in, "don't talk to her for a bit."

"*Hoi!* My bad!"

The emergency escape rocket attached to the tip of the orbiter fell away.

T plus 260 seconds. They were now at an altitude of 170 kilometers.

The pressure climbed to over 4 G. Yukari felt her limbs pressing down into her chair. Now all she could do was look at the instrument panels and wait. She wasn't even obligated to report.

4.5 G... 5 G... 6 G... 7 G...

"Just a little more."

They hit 8 G and then, like that, they were floating.

"Main booster burn finished."

There was a crisp sound as the main booster separated. On the booster, small retro-rockets fired to pull it farther away from the orbiter.

"MB separation light."

"Main booster separated. Nice job, you two!"

"Yeah. *Mangosteen*'s systems are all operational. Uh—signing off for a second."

Yukari switched her transmitter from ALWAYS ON to PUSH TO TALK. Once she was sure they couldn't hear her on the ground, she said, "Akane! We made it!"

No answer.

Yukari undid her harness and looked over at Akane's helmet.

Sleeping like an angel.

Figures...

She opened Akane's visor and patted her on the cheek.

"Akane. Akane, wake up."

"Huh...Yukari?" Her eyes fluttered open.

"Rise and shine, Akane. You're in space."

She stuck her hands out in front of her face. They floated. Akane's face lifted and she looked out the window. "The ocean! And clouds...look, the edges are rainbow colored—that must be a storm! Wow..."

She was like a child riding a train for the first time.

"Beautiful, isn't it?"

"This is amazing, Yukari. It *is* beautiful. The earth is beautiful!" Akane's eyes shone.

"Did I tell you or what!" Yukari beamed. *I'm so glad you came, Akane. To the SSA, and on this mission.*

Up here, Nellis Academy felt very far away indeed. She might have cursed the place once, but that had been enough.

"The most amazing part is when you do a spacewalk. But let's contact mission control, shall we?"

"Oh, right."

"Careful, whatever you say will stay in the log, so you don't have to mention that you fainted. Not that you'll be able to hide the medical monitor record."

"Oh..." Akane frowned. "So I did faint."

"Hey, it's okay. You were still in training, after all. So, give your first report."

"Right." Akane nodded and pressed the talk button. "Solomon Mission Control, can you read me? This is Akane on the *Mangosteen*."

"*Hoi*, Akane! How is it up there?"

"I saw a rainbow. It was gorgeous!"

"That's great. Lucky you!"

"Thanks, Matsuri. And thank everyone on the base for me."

Yukari cut in. "All right, we're preparing to adjust our orbit. Signing off."

"*Hoi*, we'll send you our program as soon as it's ready."

This was the moment of truth—the first of several, actually. Yukari carefully began a check on every system. Getting into space didn't mean you could just float around, doing nothing. The space shuttle and *Mangosteen* had to orbit the earth at a speed of over seven kilometers a second or they would fall back down to Earth. *Mangosteen* was currently in orbit at an altitude of two hundred kilometers—a full hundred kilometers below the space shuttle.

Picture a drawing of two concentric circles. The small circle is *Mangosteen's* orbit, the large circle is the space shuttle's. Now, draw an ellipsis connecting the six o'clock position on the small circle with the twelve o'clock position on the larger circle. What they had to do next was take that elliptical route from their current six o'clock position to the shuttle's twelve o'clock position, ascending the hundred-kilometer gap as they completed a half orbit of the earth.

In order to increase the altitude of their orbits, they would have to put on speed. This meant firing their thrusters just the right amount at the six o'clock position. It also meant firing their thrusters again when they reached the shuttle's twelve o'clock position, because if they didn't, they would descend on their new elliptical orbit.

The trick was to put on just enough speed to match that of the shuttle. Of course, the shuttle needed to be there at that exact time too, or the two spacecraft would never meet.

A successful rendezvous depended on two accurate thrusts at exactly the right time, landing position, speed, and direction with fantastic precision. The technology involved was an entire magnitude more complex than that required just to get into space. Miss the timing just once, and they would fall back to Earth. Yukari didn't care so much about the SSA's reputation, but she didn't want to look like a fool. Particularly because of the attention she got and the rumors that she was window dressing and all the tough work was being done by computers.

"It's my own bad luck for looking so good."

"What was that?" Akane asked.

"Nothing. You mind checking the antenna system? I've got the engine."

"Right."

The heat resistant shields on the rear of the orbiter were open, allowing the nozzles for the OMS engine they used to adjust their course while in orbit to stick out. For fuel, they used mono-methyl hydrazine and nitric quadroxide. Helium gas was used to keep pressure on the fuels and push them together when the time came.

All that was required for thrust was for the two fuels to touch, making for very accurate operation. In the end, the entire engine was controlled by a series of valves. Yukari liked to think of this job as resembling that of operating a waterworks.

A small parabolic antenna was attached to the bottom of the ship, pointing toward a TDRS, one of NASA's stationary communications satellites. By tapping into the satellite communications network, they could stay in touch with the ground no matter where they were in their orbit.

"I have confirmed a data link with the TDRS."

"Great. That should get us through to the guys on the shuttle."

"I should think so. Want to say anything to them?"

"Let's talk after we're on our elliptical orbit. I don't want to show off only to stick our feet in our mouths."

Akane chuckled nervously. "Good point."

[ACT 6]

"THERE—THAT'S THEM! It really only took them two hours after takeoff to get here," Luis remarked. He was looking through an observation window in the ceiling with binoculars. "Their orbiter looks exactly like that old Gemini module. Japan's made some progress."

"It might look the same, but that orbiter's designed to be reused even after reentry," the captain said. "It can lose a heatshield tile and still have no problem when it hits the ocean. Don't take them lightly. They're using next-gen technology compared to us." He called to Norman who was waiting in the air lock. "*Mangosteen* is three klicks below us. You finish your breathing?"

"I'm ready to go whenever."

"Well don't until they grab hold of our RMA. You don't want to take a blast from a thruster."

"I know, I know."

Just then, a childlike voice came in over the transmitter. It was a girl, speaking English with a Japanese accent.

"Space shuttle *Atlantis*, this is SSA orbiter *Mangosteen*. We have visual contact with your ship, over."

"*Mangosteen*, this is *Atlantis*. We read you loud and clear. Make your approach whenever you're ready."

"Roger. We should be finished with our rendezvous sequence in four minutes."

When they finished their apogee thrust, the two ships were in stable orbit a kilometer apart from each other.

"Sequence complete. Looks like I was only about a hundred meters or so off."

"That's pretty good."

"Don't congratulate me until I nail this docking procedure."

Yukari switched the RCS to manual mode and lowered their nose slightly. Now they could see the shuttle in their forward porthole. The shuttle was flying in a sideways orbit, its nose pointed straight toward Earth. Above the wings, the payload bay doors were open, the silver heat exchange panels glittering in the sunlight. Yukari spotted what must've been the Orpheus lodged between them.

Akane gave a little squeal despite herself. "Wow! What a beautiful ship."

"Yeah, and that's a whole kilometer away. It's pretty big." Yukari pressed the button on her maneuvering joystick. She felt a sensation like her seat pushing her from behind. "Mission control, this is *Mangosteen*. I'm beginning docking under manual control."

"*Hoi, Mangosteen*. Roger. NASA was worried you might hit them with some hydrazine. Show them how good you are, Yukari."

"Let's not forget that they're the ones who messed up here."

"I'll be sure to remind Kinoshita of that. Okay, I'm switching you to a shared channel. No more Japanese."

"Roger."

Akane switched the channel on their transmitter. "*Atlantis*, this is *Mangosteen*. We are three hundred meters away and approaching."

"Roger, *Mangosteen*. Can you see our RMA?"

"Very well, thanks."

The remote manipulation arm was extended out straight from near the nose of the shuttle like the mast on a sailing ship.

The *Mangosteen* had its own smaller RMA. They would use theirs to grab the tip of the shuttle's arm, pass down a rope, and they'd be docked.

"See how they extended their RMA all the way out? They don't trust us."

"I was wondering if that's what it meant."

"They don't want us blasting their precious shuttle with our thrusters. Either that, or they're afraid I'm going to run into them. Wimps."

"Well, as long as you're sure we can pull this off."

"What, now you don't trust me, either?"

Akane shook her head. "I'm the one who's going to be operating our RMA while you pilot."

"No problem, Akane. The real RMA's just like the simulator. You stretch it out and grab when the moment comes. Don't think about it too much, just do it."

"Stretch it out and grab," Akane repeated to herself. "Okay."

They were almost on top of the shuttle now. Yukari fired several short blasts, bringing their orbiter into position close to the tip of the shuttle's RMA and stopping it there.

"Nice job, *Mangosteen*. We won't have to do anything at this rate."

That would be the shuttle's RMA operator. He would have been standing by to chase after them with his arm if they had missed.

"Thanks," Yukari replied. "Time to shake hands."

Akane grabbed the RMA joystick with her right hand. Her left hand rested on the mode selector. The folded arm inside their nose cone extended, reaching forward. In all, *Mangosteen*'s arm was only 2.4 meters long—far shorter than the shuttle's fifteen-meter arm, but more agile for it.

The two fingers on the arm approached their target, a flat panel attached to the shuttle's RMA.

"That's right, a little more."

Because their orbiter was so small, just moving the RMA had the effect of moving their ship slightly in the opposite direction. Akane, however, was giving a textbook performance, keeping the arm motion lateral so that any reverse momentum would pass directly through the orbiter's center of gravity to avoid producing spin.

"Think I should grab it now?"

"Go for it!"

She pressed the button, and the metal fingers closed precisely on their target.

"I did it!" Akane pressed the button down further. "And...it's locked on."

"Great stuff! *Atlantis*, we have your RMA. We're preparing to exit the orbiter."

"Excellent work. I'll admit, we didn't expect it to go this smoothly."

There are benefits to being small and agile, Yukari thought.

The two girls removed their harnesses and put on the backpacks stored in the backs of their seats. The backpacks—each only the size of a daypack—contained a small life-support system and transmitter. After attaching cables to their suits, they were ready.

Yukari spent an extra moment carefully rechecking all of Akane's gear.

"This is another one of those moments of truth. Be relaxed, but cautious; quick, but not rushed."

"Okay."

"Also, there'll be plenty of time for gazing at Earth later so don't do it now. Once you're outside, orient yourself to the shuttle. Think of us as being above the shuttle, like a pennant flying on a flagpole. Once you're outside, try *not* to spin around if you can avoid it. It's very easy to get disoriented."

"Okay."

The two attached Kevlar fiber lifelines and lowered their airtight visors on their helmets.

"Com test."

"Loud and clear."

Yukari ejected the air from the orbiter and opened the hatch. "Here we go."

"Right behind you."

Over on the space shuttle, the entire crew was pressed up to the rear observation window.

"Look, they're coming out already!"

"I don't believe it! It's only been ten minutes since they finished docking."

They all knew the schedule, but hearing about it and seeing it actually happen were two different things. Whenever a spacewalk was required on the shuttle, it took at least two hours just to get ready. Because NASA space suits maintained a low pressure, the astronauts had to breathe pure oxygen for a considerable length of time to remove the nitrogen in their bloodstreams in preparation for their new environment.

The first astronaut came out of the *Mangosteen* and made her way around the nose. Pulling a rope from the pouch at her waist, she threaded it through the RMA, firmly anchoring it to their ship in a matter of moments.

"Did you see that rope work? She just tied a sheep-shank in space!"

"Never mind that," Luis said. "Check out those space suits! They look like Eva over there—"

"Ava Gardner?"

"No. I'll loan you the anime when we get back."

The second astronaut emerged. This one moved more slowly than the first, carefully making her way along the hull.

Both astronauts made their way to the shuttle's RMA and came halfway down. Holding on to the arm with one hand, the first astronaut faced the shuttle. "Hello, *Atlantis*. Can you see us?"

"See you? We can't take our eyes off you. You look like angels up there."

"I'm the one with my left hand raised—Captain Yukari Morita."

"Welcome to *Atlantis*, Yukari. I'm Captain Wayne Berkheimer."

"Nice to meet you, Captain."

"Call me Wayne. Who's that next to you?"

"Er...this is mission specialist Akane Miura. Hello."

"Nice to meet you, Akane."

"You can tell us apart by the stripes on our space suits. Mine are pink, and Akane's are blue."

"Roger that, you both look great."

"We're going to begin retrieval, if that's all right."

"Hold on, we're sending someone out. Norman, can you go show the angels what they need to know?"

"Roger. I'm heading out the air lock now."

By the time Norman made it outside, the two girls were already on the Orpheus's upper-stage engine. They had attached their lifelines from the *Mangosteen* to the bottom of the RMA in favor of a single lifeline strung between them.

Norman headed over to Orpheus, though by the time he had walked the seven- or eight-meter distance, one of the girls was already going inside the engine structure.

"Hey, wait up. You Akane?"

Akane pulled her head out of the truss around the engine, looking. She jerked visibly when she saw him.

"Something wrong?"

"Sorry. I just didn't expect you to be so big."

"What, me? Don't worry, I don't bite. I'm heading over there."

Norman slowly crawled up the upper-stage engine cover. Yukari stuck out her hand, reeling him in.

"Thanks."

Compared to these two, I'm like one of those walking cartoon characters at Disneyland, Norman thought.

The two other astronauts looked frighteningly small and thin to the American. Their waists were barely bigger around than one of his arms in the space suit. And while he looked like the Michelin man, they were *shapely*. You didn't expect to see curves like that in the payload bay of a space shuttle flying at three hundred kilometers above the surface of the earth.

Their golden reflective visors were up, so he could see their faces—*like dolls*, he thought.

"The valve assembly is inside there. See the gap on the engine side in the center of the ring?"

"So it's in there just behind the helium tank, right?" Akane asked.

"That's right. How'd you know?"

"I'm a quick study."

"All right, well, be careful. Every single tank in there is dangerous."

"I'm aware of that."

"Shall we get started, Akane?" Yukari asked. "Let's go in and check things out first. Take it easy. It's more tangled in there than it was in the CG simulation."

"Right."

Akane was getting used to extravehicular activity by now.

In the skintight space suit she wore, it was hardly any more difficult than scuba diving. But Yukari was right. Compared to the training video they had seen, the real engine structure had all kinds of small protrusions here and there. This wouldn't be easy.

Akane slid inside the truss.

"A little more to the left, Akane."

"Got it."

"That's right. Keep going."

"My head is close to the center now. I'm going to try swiveling."

A few moments later, Akane reported that she'd found the valve assembly. "It's about another meter in there—huh?"

"What is it? I can't see very well."

"My backpack's hung up on something."

"Careful, Akane. Take it easy. Don't move too quickly."

"Okay...I'm going to try swiveling again."

"Any luck?"

"Ack. It's another fifty centimeters or so."

"Don't push it. Let's try a different approach," Norman offered. "Akane, come out for now."

"I'm coming." Akane pushed herself out feet first. Norman could see beads of sweat on her face.

"There's something sticking out halfway in, about the size of a fist. I keep getting hung up on that."

"Would a tool work?" Norman asked. "We have a probe about the same size as a back scratcher."

"No, a straight probe won't work. There are too many twists."

"Hmm."

"Wait, I know how I can do it," Akane said suddenly. "I'll take off my backpack."

"What?" Norman gasped. "Did you just say you're going to take off your backpack?"

"No, Akane, I'll do it," Yukari said.

"You can't take your backpack off! That's like instant death!"

"No it's not," Yukari said. "Our backpacks have quick disconnect valves on them. You can remove them in a vacuum and not lose any air."

"But the air inside your helmet won't last more than a minute!"

"That's nothing for a skin diver. I'll be in and out in a flash."

"But what if you got caught on something—"

"Don't worry. I can do this. Akane, you guide me from here."

"No, Yukari, please. Let me do it."

"Akane—"

"Really, I'm confident I can do it."

"We won't be able to communicate. You won't have your transmitter."

"I'll increase my oxygen and saturate before I go in. I should be good for three minutes. If I don't come out before then, haul me out with a lifeline."

Yukari stared at Akane's face through her visor.

Those eyes—like still water. She can do this. "Okay. Go for it."

"Whoa, Captain, you hearing this? I don't think we can let them—"

Wayne cut off Norman's protest. "Yukari, I'm not sure what SSA safety standards are like, but the danger of this operation is unprecedented. Are you sure you can just let her go in there?"

"Actually, at the SSA, we switch backpacks outside the ship all the time. If you just think of this as an extension of that, it's really no big deal."

"But we have to consider the possibility that she'll take more time than we expect—"

"It's no more dangerous than skin diving, Captain. Do they not allow skin diving in America?"

There was a long pause before the captain responded.

"Fine, we'll just have to trust that you know what you're doing."

Yukari nodded and Akane turned to crank up the oxygen levels on her life support. She began taking rapid breaths.

"Don't take too much, you'll get high."

"I know."

Akane deftly removed her backpack and attached a light to her wrist.

Yukari touched her helmet to Akane's and spoke. "What day is it?"

"Thursday, on the Solomon Islands."

"Great. Be careful in there."

"Will do."

With a twist like a mermaid breaking through the water, Akane disappeared back into the truss. Yukari started the chronograph on her wrist. She looked up to find Norman staring at her. He said nothing. They both waited, breathlessly.

When the needle on her chronograph had gone around twice, she saw something moving inside the truss.

A white glove emerged—holding the valve assembly.

"She made it!"

Yukari reached out and grabbed the assembly. Handing it to Norman, she quickly reached back and grabbed Akane's hand. Akane slid smoothly out and hurriedly reattached her backpack. Yukari could hear her rapid breaths once she had the electrical cable reattached.

"Are you okay?"

"It was a lot—" she took a heaving breath, "—it was a lot easier than the first time."

"Ha ha!" Yukari cheered and gave Akane a big hug. "A complete success! That's my grade-A student!"

Akane laughed. "I'm just glad I'm not getting in the way."

"We can't even bring a change of clothes on the orbiter. Why would we waste all that space on something that just got in the way?"

"Good point!"

The girls were rattling on in Japanese when Captain Berkheimer cut in.

"*Arigato*—sorry, that's all the Japanese I know."

"Oh, sorry."

"No, not at all. You've really helped us out. It's not much, but would you like to join us on the middeck for a welcoming party? I've already gotten permission from Solomon."

They weren't initially scheduled to visit the shuttle at all, to avoid interfering with their mission.

"We'd love to join you," Yukari said without a moment's hesitation.

[ACT 7]

THEY PASSED THROUGH a circular air lock and arrived on the middeck. There was a line of white lockers in front of them, three sleeping berths on the right with a small galley on the side. On the left was a toilet and access hatch for the decks above and below.

In the remaining space, three men waited in T-shirts and shorts.

Yukari and Akane took off their helmets and held them at their sides.

A cheer went up. They always got this reaction when they took off their helmets in front of men—something about it was particularly enchanting, apparently, though Yukari had never figured out exactly what.

"Welcome to shuttle *Atlantis*," the captain said, extending his hand. He was in his early fifties, with a long face and rough whiskers on his chin. Yukari would have taken him for a British gentleman on his day off, but seeing as how he was a shuttle captain, he was most likely a former U.S. military test pilot or of similar stock.

"Excellent work out there," he said. "You did in five minutes what we couldn't do in five days. My hat's off to you."

"Not at all," Yukari said pleasantly, "but I will say I was impressed by my mission specialist's work. Allow me to introduce our new rookie at SSA, Akane Miura."

"No, really, it was nothing," Akane blurted as she shook each of the men's hands in turn.

Next it was the shuttle crew's turn to introduce themselves.

The pilot, Luis, was thirty-seven years old, ex–Air Force. Something about his eyebrows made him look a bit like the actor Koji Ishizaka, and one of the first things he asked them was which anime was the most popular right now in Japan.

Akane had no idea, and when Yukari suggested *Chimaera Ball Z* off-the-cuff, he informed her that it had already been canceled.

Gordon, the shuttle MS, was thirty-one years old, an aerospace engineer for an airline company who'd switched over to NASA. He was a handsome fellow with blond hair and an anxious look in his eye, despite his relief that the valve assembly had been retrieved. It was his mishap with the RMA that had lost it in the first place.

The two girls were offered juice in tubes, biscuits, and freeze-dried ice cream. A couple of the men offered them gum and chocolate out of their personal lockers. Nothing up here was particularly tasty, but the variety was welcome.

Norman emerged from the air lock. He was a big man with a crew cut. Had they been standing on the ground, Yukari would have only come up to his chest.

Though he had taken off his helmet and backpack, he was still in his bulky space suit. The five spread out to the floor and the ceiling to make room in the suddenly crowded middeck.

"Sorry we started without you. Good work out there," the captain said to him.

"I didn't do anything. They're the ones you should thank," Norman said gruffly.

Seen from this close, his space suit looked incredibly unwieldy. The chest was like a barrel wrapped in cloth. His arms and legs were tubes, completely obliterating the human form beneath.

"You look like a sumo wrestler," Yukari said, earning a smoldering look from Norman.

"If I had a suit like yours, I'd be able to keep up with you up there."

"Maybe, though you're so big as it is I doubt you would have been able to get inside that truss."

There was silence in the middeck.

The captain cleared his throat. "So, you two, want to check out the cockpit?"

"Oh yes, that'd be great!" Akane said eagerly.

"Why not," Yukari said with obvious disinterest. "Just the thing—technology older than I am. It'll be like being in a museum."

Akane glared at her, but Yukari pretended not to notice.

The captain led them through a hole in the ceiling onto the upper deck. Though photographs and video made it look larger, in reality, the cockpit was small—roughly the size of a truck cabin with a sleeper behind the seats.

"As you can see, everything but the floors and ceilings are covered with instrumentation. Everything up front is the flight controls—it's pretty much the same as a commercial airliner. The right side is for mission operations and the left is for payload operations. In the back we've got the RMA control and the docking controls."

"It's a two-seater," Akane noted.

"That's right. The only people that actually have to sit up here are the pilots when the shuttle is in flight mode. See the footrests? You can adjust the height on those, so even someone your size could fit snugly."

"That was a smart design."

"We have to consider the range of people that come up on the space shuttle. Different sizes, different races, different religions. We're set up to take them all."

"Unlike the SSA, you mean," Yukari said.

"Yukari!" Akane was visibly angry now. She spoke Japanese. "Why are you saying things like that? What did these guys ever do to you?"

"Nothing."

"So why the attitude?"

"It's just in my nature to rebel in front of an authority like NASA."

Akane blinked. "Okay, but aren't we supposed to be emphasizing goodwill and international relations up here in space?"

"Man, you really are a grade-A student! You talk like a textbook sometimes, Akane. We're leaving here in just a little bit anyway. Who cares if you get along with these people?"

The captain watched them, a look of concern on his face. Akane didn't think he understood Japanese, but their tone of voice was probably information enough for him to make some assumptions about what they were saying.

"Well, I think it's important to be nice to other people. It's an opportunity to make friends—you never know how the people you meet might help you in the future," Akane said quietly.

"You don't say."

"Opportunity only knocks once, Yukari."

"It's only opportunity if they're worthwhile people. Meeting some bum probably isn't going to get you very far."

"Just think, I met you, and now I'm up here."

"Oh, so that's where you're going with this?"

Akane nodded. "Remember when you told me to get on the helicopter? I was terrified. But I just did it. I had the feeling like that was the start of something." She smiled a little. "I think I've gotten better at meeting people since then. And being *nice* to them. Especially when I think of what possibilities might lie in store for me."

"Well, I call that being a goody-two-shoes."

"I'm fine with being a goody-two-shoes," Akane said with a guileless smile.

Yukari looked off into space and sighed. *Why do I always get the insanely optimistic ones for partners?*

"Fine. So I should go apologize to Norman, is that what you want?"

Akane nodded cheerfully.

Yukari excused herself and went back down to the middeck. There she found Luis and Gordon eating Snickers bars.

"Did Norman go somewhere?"

"He's pre-breathing in the air lock," Luis told her.

"He's going out again?"

"Yep. He has to put on the new valve that you brought with you."

"Pre-breathing takes about two hours, right?"

"That's right."

Wait, he didn't come back in here just for our welcoming party, did he?

"Did you have something to talk to him about? You can get him on the intercom."

"No...no, that's all right."

I'm sure he came back to replenish the oxygen and his backup. That has to be it.

"So, Yukari," Luis said, "want to exchange souvenirs? We do with the Russians whenever they dock. Here, here's mine."

Luis pulled a cloth emblem out of his pocket. It was a special badge for the Orpheus Mission.

"Wow, that's nice. But I don't have anything like that to give you."

"Oh, doesn't have to be anything special. A notebook or a pen, anything."

"I might have a pen." Yukari rummaged in her waist pouch and found a Fischer ballpoint pen. "Here. It even has the Solomon Space Association logo on it. How's this?"

"Ooh! That's great!" The pilot seemed genuinely happy.

Just then, the captain called down. "Think you can come up here, Yukari? Dr. O'Reilly wants to talk to you."

"O'Reilly?" Yukari asked as she made her way to the upper deck.

"Chief designer on the Orpheus Project. He wants to thank you personally."

Now this is a person worth meeting, Yukari thought. Yukari and Akane held on to the backrest of the pilot seats in the cockpit and positioned themselves facing the intercom.

"You did all the work. I'll leave this one up to you," Yukari said to Akane.

"Are you sure?"

"Aren't you the goody-two-shoes who likes meeting people? Especially scientists?"

Akane nodded and pressed the talk button. "This is Akane Miura on *Atlantis*. Hello, Dr. O'Reilly."

"Ah, you're the one who took off her backpack and retrieved that valve?"

"That's right."

"Thank you! Thank you so much!" His voice wavered, making the end of his words a mess of static. "I'm afraid I can't express just how grateful I am to you."

Akane cleared her throat. "I think I understand, Doctor. I heard that the Orpheus probe had been put in storage for a whole decade. Is that true?"

"Yes, the project officially started over twenty-two years ago now."

Akane swallowed. "That's an awfully long time."

"Pluto isn't as exciting as the other planets, you see. I don't know how many times our budget got cut. And then, after the *Challenger* explosion—"

"I see."

"We needed a powerful liquid fuel engine for the Orpheus's prolusion system—Pluto is a long way off, as you know. After the *Challenger* accident, it became more difficult to carry that kind of fuel up in the shuttle. Safety regulations and all. Of course I understand but... I'm sorry, I don't mean to bore you."

"Not at all, Doctor. I find it fascinating," Akane said.

"Well, it's only been recently that Pluto has garnered more attention. Being small and frozen, it's not as exciting as the other planets, you see. In fact, there are some who consider it a Kuiper belt object and not a planet at all. Yet if it is this, then surely it is a representative of the belt, and therefore worthy of study."

"The Kuiper belt... That's where comets come from, right?" Yukari asked.

"One of the places, yes!"

The Kuiper belt formed a great ring of innumerable celestial objects just outside of Pluto's orbit, all too distant and small to see from Earth, even with a decent telescope. Most of them just sat out there frozen in space for an eternity, but when something happened to kick one out of orbit, it would plummet toward the sun, becoming a beautiful streaming-tailed comet.

Though some comets came from even farther afield, those with a relatively frequent orbit were usually thought to have originated in the Kuiper belt, where Pluto stood as lord of the gates.

"So Pluto's like the big boss of the comets."

"That's what I want to find out. Even Voyager missed Pluto on its survey of the outer planets. It's the last large object in the solar system that hasn't been studied from relatively up close. If Orpheus makes it there, it will be the first probe to observe Pluto from space local to it. I'm sure we'll see some astronomy textbooks rewritten."

"When is it scheduled to arrive?"

"Oh, the trip will take twelve years. It takes even light a good four hours to cover the distance, after all. How old will you be then?" the professor asked.

"Twenty-eight."

"Splendid. I'm jealous. Until recently, I had given up hope that I would ever see a close-up image of Pluto in my lifetime. But now I've made up my mind," he said with rising cheer. "As of today, I'm giving up doughnuts and cigarettes! This is all thanks to you, you know," he added. "Thank you ever so much."

"You're welcome, and I hope I can see those pictures with you someday."

The transmission was over, but Akane remained facing the speaker, tears welling weightlessly in the corners of her eyes.

[ACT 8]

THEY USUALLY WENT home immediately after their work was done, but now the girls had to wait until their orbit took them back to the ocean near the Solomon Islands. With the abruptness of their mission, there hadn't been time to properly mobilize retrieval teams.

That would be another eleven hours, or another twenty-four if they wanted to avoid a splashdown at night. Now came the tough part: killing time. Since they were already there, Yukari and Akane decided to spend that time lounging in the shuttle. The two girls sat by the rear observation window, nibbling on freeze-dried strawberries and observing the progress toward the Orpheus launch.

Norman and Gordon were out there now in their space suits, fiddling with the engine and making adjustments.

"This is incredibly nerve-racking to watch. I mean, it takes them minutes just to pick up a new tool," Yukari muttered.

"It's not their fault."

"I know that. It's just, it's hard to sit here and do nothing. I want to be out there helping them."

"I'm not sure they'd appreciate that. Guys don't like being helped."

"It's a little late for that," Yukari said, but she understood well enough. This was their chance to reclaim their honor. Even she knew better than to take that away from them.

In truth, the NASA astronauts' patience and stamina were astounding. Each trip outside lasted several hours, and while they had water and some candy inside their helmets to keep their energy up, they never took anything like a break. That, and just moving your arm in one of those space suits was like doing a rep with a heavy dumbbell in weight training.

I could never do what they're doing, Yukari thought.

Disaster struck five hours after the girls' arrival on the shuttle. They were on middeck at the time. The intercom monitoring the two astronauts' conversation squawked with static.

"What the hell—"

"Get down!"

Akane and Yukari quickly made their way to the upper deck to find the captain and Luis glued to the rear observation window.

"You two okay?" the captain shouted into his intercom. Yukari peeked over his shoulder at the window and her mouth dropped open.

Orpheus and the upper-stage engine were gone.

The payload bay was entirely empty, save for Norman and Gordon who were drifting around just outside of it.

"We're okay." It was Norman. "I felt a little gas pressure, but life support's all good. Just, we lost it. Godamnit! We lost it!"

"Try to calm down, Norman. I want you back in the ship. We'll think of a way to deal with this."

"What happened?" Yukari asked.

"The upper-stage engine fired. Luckily, no one was hurt."

"What, it exploded?"

"No, it *fired*. Something caused it to start a thrust."

A call came in from the Johnson Space Center in Houston. "*Atlantis*, this is Houston. We saw what happened. Do you have a report?"

"Houston, we have an accident. No injuries or life lost. I'm bringing our two men outside back into the shuttle. I'll send more details once I've had a chance to talk with them."

"The engine burn's stopped," Luis said. He was standing by the window, tracking Orpheus with a pair of binoculars. "It was a controlled burn, looks like—and it's gone. I've lost visual contact."

"Norman, you copy?" the captain asked.

"We can talk. We're inside the air lock."

"Did you check the tag? Can Orpheus be remotely controlled?"

"No remote control. The safety tag was still on."

"Can you confirm, Gordon?"

"I saw the tag with my own eyes. We checked it before releasing the restraints on the probe."

"Any idea how the engine could've fired?"

"You got me."

"Houston, this is *Atlantis*. Something caused Orpheus's engines to fire while the safety tag was still on. It was a controlled burn, lasting roughly three minutes. That's all we know at present."

"Roger. We're checking Orpheus's telemetry. We'll let you know as soon as we find something."

Yukari went back to middeck. She wanted to know what was going on, but now was not the time to interrupt. The air lock hatch opened and Norman came out. He closed the hatch behind him and found the intercom. "You're clear to come in, Gordon."

The nameplate on the left arm of the space suit was scorched black and half of his visor was clouded.

"Norman! Are you all right?" Yukari asked.

"I'm fine."

His face dripped with sweat, and there was a hard look in his eyes. And something else too—anger. Norman began undoing his gear.

"Can I help with anything?" Yukari asked.

"Nothing I want your help with."

"I'm okay with sweat, and urine."

He glanced at her. "Then hold up the bottom half of my suit."

Yukari got a grip on Norman's legs while he began undoing the connector with the torso. The space suit split into two halves. He took off his liquid cooling garment until he was in his undershirt and MAG. The letters stood for Maximum Absorbency Garment—basically a glorified diaper astronauts wore during liftoff, landing, and extravehicular activities to absorb urine. The smell of sweat filled the deck.

"Are you injured? Any bruises?"

"I'm okay. The blast only hit me for a second," Norman said as he slipped on his shipwear. "Any word on Orpheus?"

"The burn went for three minutes, and by then it was out of sight."

"Three minutes?" Norman bit his lip.

"What does it mean?"

"A three-minute burn isn't enough to break the probe from orbit, but it makes it very difficult—if not impossible—for the shuttle to retrieve it."

"Can I ask another question?"

"What?"

"What's the safety tag?"

"It's a nonconductive strip that keeps the controller from accidentally activating the engine. Orpheus is wirelessly controllable, but we keep the tag on until it's completely prepared for launch to avoid an accident. As long as the tag's on there, nothing like this should ever have happened."

"So you can't remote control it and slow it down now?"

"Most likely not. You'd think if it was malfunctioning, we might have a chance, but that's too much to hope for." Norman turned to go to the upper deck.

"Norman—"

"Later."

Yukari's mouth snapped shut.

Akane came down the hatch as soon as Norman was through.

"Oh, no, Yukari! What do we do?" She had tears in her eyes again, like a dam ready to crack wide open.

"What do you mean?"

"It's *my* fault. When I went into the engine space to retrieve the valve I must have broken something. That's what happened! How will I ever face Dr. O'Reilly?"

"H-hey!" Akane pressed her face to Yukari's chest and cried.

"Just hold on. Do you remember breaking anything?"

"No...but I'm sure I touched the truss in at least a few places. It was hard to avoid."

"It's not that easy to break an engine, Akane. You know they're built to withstand quite a bit of heat and vibration."

Akane nodded, sniffing.

"There's still hope. Just try to stay calm. I want to see those 'I can do anything' eyes of yours, okay?"

Akane stopped crying.

"Or else I'll have to take you off active duty."

Akane hiccuped for a little while longer, then gave a nod.

An hour later, the captain called the entire crew to middeck.

"Let's go over what we know. First of all, just so there's no false hope, you should know that the situation is not looking good. The engine burn came when Orpheus was nearly ready for launch. It's now fallen into a roughly three-thousand-kilometer-high elliptical orbit.

"That's not all that different from its scheduled orbit, so if we could operate it remotely, it might be possible to refire the engine and send it on its way to Pluto. The fuel loss from the burn was still within tolerance levels.

"However, we've been unable to establish remote control over the probe from the ground. This is likely due to the safety tag still being attached.

"Furthermore, I've just heard from Houston about why this happened. While they can't be certain until they actually see the probe, it seems likely that something happened during an un-scheduled engine test before launch. Apparently, one of the tech-nicians on the ground purposefully shorted the control circuits in order to fire the engines with the safety tag still on.

"Time is tight, they needed to do the test, and removing the safety tag requires a lot of paperwork. Furthermore, the technician has admitted he has no memory of removing the jumper he used to short the firing circuits."

While the captain spoke, Yukari was watching Akane's expression.

At first she looked relieved. But that relief soon shifted to quiet anger. The other crewmembers were making fists with their hands and cursing under their breaths.

"If we were able to rendezvous with Orpheus, the solution would be simple. All we'd have to do is remove the safety tag and the jumper wire from the circuit. However—" the captain paused to let his men prepare themselves for the bad news. "As I mentioned, the orbiter is on an elliptical orbit with an apogee of roughly three thousand kilometers. We don't have enough fuel to accelerate *Atlantis* enough for a rendezvous with the probe. Not to mention the shuttle has an altitude limit of one thousand kilometers."

"So we're done here," Luis said quietly with a shrug. "Let's go home, have a few beers, and forget any of this ever happened."

"That's looking like the best course of action," the captain admitted, shaking his head. "Incidentally—" He turned to Yukari. "What's *Mangosteen*'s altitude limit?"

"Eight hundred kilometers."

"As I thought."

There was silence for a few moments.

No matter which craft they used, neither of them would be able to reach Orpheus. Though the probe would pass through the shuttle's orbit at its closest point to Earth, there would be a speed differential of nearly 640 meters per second. Even if they could reach the same exact spot, without matching speeds there'd be no rendezvous.

Akane spoke. "So what happens to Orpheus?"

"It's pretty low when it approaches the earth. Eventually it will bump up against the atmosphere, which will slow it down, and after several orbits it will plunge."

"And what about after we return to Earth? Will there be no chance to save it after that?"

"Unfortunately, no."

"Then, Captain," Akane said, "I have a suggestion."

The captain looked up at her.

"Neither of our ships on its own can catch Orpheus. But what if we combined the ships?"

"What are you suggesting?"

"Well, we could put *Mangosteen* inside *Atlantis* and accelerate as fast as the shuttle will go. Then we release *Mangosteen* and accelerate with her."

"Yes, but—"

"It's an addition problem," Luis said, shaking his head. "One thousand plus eight hundred doesn't equal three thousand."

"Actually, it does," Akane said. "What you're saying would be true if the orbits were circular, but in order to match an elliptical orbit, we only need to accelerate half of the distance between us."

"Wait, you're right! We could hit an apogee of thirty-six hundred kilometers!"

"Correct. It helps if you think in terms of velocity instead of altitude."

"But hold on," the captain interjected. "We need fuel to adjust our orbital plane, but we also need fuel to get back home."

"Actually, the orbital plane won't change that much. And both of our ships can handle atmosphere. You won't need much fuel to get back."

"What's *Mangosteen*'s mass?" Norman asked.

"Roughly two tons, including crew."

"The shuttle weighs seventy thousand kilograms. That's barely different than flying with an empty bay."

"We'll fit in the payload bay nicely too," Yukari said. "Even at its widest point, our orbiter's diameter is only three meters."

"So we've established that theoretically, this is possible," Gordon said, leaning forward. "As long as we got the rendezvous timing perfect."

"It is possible. It's totally possible!" Akane said.

"Now, hold on. Just *hold on*," the captain said. "Loading a space shuttle with an unscheduled cargo and accelerating has never been attempted before. This isn't some eighteen-wheeler we're driving up here. If that orbiter were to, say, topple in the bay midflight we could be looking at a catastrophic explosion.

"Also, the shuttle needs an airport in order to land. If we change our course and have to make an emergency landing, we'll be looking at a far worse disaster than just losing Orpheus. Not to mention that a height of three thousand kilometers hasn't been attempted since the Apollo missions. There's no telling what could happen up there."

"And we'll find out as much as we can! Call the Solomon base and the Johnson Space Center and have them plan the whole thing out!" Akane said, a mounting strength in her voice. "If you keep bringing up why we can't succeed, it just means you aren't up to doing it!"

The captain raised an eyebrow at her.

"It's like she says," Yukari joined in. "We're ready to go to three thousand kilometers or thirty thousand kilometers, whatever it takes. As long as you're up to it."

The captain shook his head, then got on the intercom for the space transmission network. "Houston and Solomon, this is *Atlantis*. Do you copy?"

"*Atlantis*, this is Houston, we hear you loud and clear."

"*Hoi, Atlantis*. Solomon here."

"We need you to look into something for us. We have a possible way to rescue Orpheus. The idea's from the SSA's Miura, and it's a bit...radical."

[ACT 9]

BACK IN THE control center at the SSA, Nasuda listened attentively to Captain Berkheimer talk. When he was finished, Nasuda practically howled with delight. "She might have fainted, but Akane's got what it takes! Have our communications group send Houston whatever information they need. Kinoshita, you divide up everything else that needs to be done."

Kinoshita wasted no time. "I want the navigational team calculating an orbit. Go from the moment *Mangosteen* separates from the shuttle and try to predict as many variables as you can.

"I want the orbiter systems team figuring out how we can mount *Mangosteen* inside the shuttle. Whatever it is, it will have to be able to withstand three hundred kilograms at 0.1 G acceleration. Work up a chart of anchor points on our orbiter and any anchoring materials we might have and send it on to Houston. They're calling the shots on this one, so whatever they need, they get.

"Medical team, I want you to do some modeling on Yukari and Akane's life support systems. Remember they'll be going to three thousand kilometers.

"One last thing, and this goes for all of you. We're working in lockstep with Houston on this. I want you to share data and any ideas, no matter how far-fetched they might seem. Communication, work on setting up contact people from each team to facilitate this."

The relationship between an orbiter and ground control is a bit like the relationship between the bridge and the deck on an old large-scale sea vessel. The lower deck was where all the crew worked, and the bridge backed them up. On the water, both were in the same boat, but as space on orbiters was limited, astronauts left the bridge back home. Though space jockeys didn't like to acknowledge it, the real captain of a spaceflight was on the ground. Either way, constant contact and communication between the two was vital, especially during crises.

The response at the Johnson Space Center in Houston, Texas, was little different from that of Solomon Mission Control.

"That little girl up there is upping the ante in a big way on us," mission director George Grant muttered. What got him most was not that it was a bad idea, but that the situation forced him to take it very seriously.

Once they acknowledged the possibility, however slim, that it might work, they couldn't afford to not take it seriously. Grant himself was ready to do whatever was required to get Orpheus back under control.

The biggest hurdle they had to pass was safety regulations. Everything about this plan was going to push both crew and equipment to their theoretical limits. Just getting the shuttle by itself up to an altitude near two thousand kilometers would require using most of its remaining fuel. And then they had to factor in the strange, tropical cargo it would be carrying.

In order to calculate the amount of fuel required for the shuttle's return, they would have to assume a worst-case scenario in which they were still carrying *Mangosteen* after a launch failure. Was saving an unmanned exploratory probe worth this kind of risk?

George's mind went back to the *Apollo* 13 disaster.

It was already thirty years ago when it happened: the oxygen tank on a spacecraft bound for the moon exploded, and though they were short on fuel, electricity, and air, somehow they managed to get the astronauts back home safely.

At the time, George had been a twenty-year-old recent hire at NASA, but he still remembered going for sleepless days and nights hunched over his IBM 360 making and remaking orbital calculations. No one could've predicted what happened, but they had made it through by using what they had on hand to make the impossible possible.

George was proud to have been part of the effort to bring the *Apollo* 13 crew back home. That pride had kept him at NASA all these long years.

Well, let's do what we can do.

As a senior engineer, George was quite adept at making rough calculations in his head.

Orpheus has an orbital frequency of one hour fifty-nine minutes.

Atlantis *has an orbit of one hour thirty minutes.*

It was roughly a ratio of 4:3. Once *Atlantis* had gone around four times and Orpheus three times, the two would meet. If somehow before that moment they could accelerate *Mangosteen* to 640 meters a second, they would be able to rendezvous with Orpheus. The acceleration would have to happen in two steps, with the separation of the orbiter from the shuttle between them.

They couldn't leave this one entirely to the nav computers; it was too complex.

Already an hour had passed since the accidental engine burn.

So, what, I only have five hours left to make this happen?

George picked up the phone and dialed the person in charge of mock-ups down at the training center. Previously, they had constructed life-sized models of *Atlantis* and Orpheus for use in prelaunch training.

"I need you guys to work on something right away. I'm going to be accelerating *Atlantis* with the SSA's *Mangosteen* orbiter in her payload bay. You should be receiving specs on *Mangosteen* any moment now. The bad news is, you only have five hours—no, make that four and a half."

"We're on it." The engineer on the other side of the line thought for a moment. "Might be able to use the platform we put in there for Orpheus."

No waffling, no extraneous questions. I love working with professionals, George thought. For the first time in a long while, he felt genuine excitement stirring in his chest.

[ACT 10]

TWO HOURS LATER there was a general assembly of the crew on the middeck of *Atlantis*.

They had all clipped on intercom mics, getting ready for the next communication with ground control—the communication that would determine whether or not they were going to try to save Orpheus.

Norman and Gordon had already changed into their space suits and were pre-breathing to get ready for the next round of extravehicular operations if it came to that.

"Solomon and Houston have an early report for us," the captain told them. "If we like the sound of what they're saying, then we'll go ahead with Akane's plan. Let's hear what Houston has to say first."

"This is George Grant speaking," the voice said over the intercom. "Mission director at Houston. I'd like to share our results with you. Though our flight safety committee expressed considerable concern, they concluded that we should go ahead with the operation. Speaking only of the shuttle's safety, we predict no critical danger. They had one condition, however. They want the SSA astronauts to perform *Mangosteen*'s separation."

Yukari responded immediately. "That was our intention from the start."

"Thank you, Yukari. We'll share what details we were able to work out by fax. Over and out."

This was a surprising decision coming from the usually very conservative NASA. Yukari wasn't sure what dealings had gone on behind the scenes, but it was clear that damage control was part of the equation. So far, the SSA had been showing NASA up, and they didn't want to lose even more credibility by failing to reclaim their errant probe.

Yukari looked around at the faces of the shuttle crew. They looked determined, ready to do whatever they had to.

"*Atlantis*? This is Solomon." It was Matsuri. "We looked into Akane's plan as well."

"Go ahead, Solomon."

"Well, we don't think it will be impossible to properly stage *Mangosteen* inside the shuttle and rendezvous with Orpheus. Your splashdown point will be off the coast of Chile. Our recovery team won't be able to make it there in time, but the U.S. Navy have a cruiser nearby, and they've agreed to help. There's just one problem."

"What is it, Matsuri?" Yukari asked.

"*Hoi*, I'll have our flight surgeon explain."

Satsuki Asahikawa came on the intercom. "Listen up, you two. The problem is with radiation exposure. If you take *Mangosteen* up to Orpheus's current orbit, you'll be passing through the Van Allen belt close to the equator. There's a lot of radiation focused there."

"Is it dangerous?"

"It's not fatal, but it's a lot more radiation than any X-ray technician would ever dream of subjecting you to. Compounding the problem is the fact that both you and Akane are of childbearing age."

"So what's the bottom line?"

"As your physician, I can't allow you to stay up there for more than a single orbit."

"So you mean we have to do the rendezvous and all our work on the orbiter and reentry in the space of two hours?"

"That's right. If you can't pull that off, I'm afraid we have to cancel the mission. The radiation is highest at just around three thousand kilometers. You'll hit that halfway through your first orbit, so you'll need to finish all your work outside the ship by then. Though the protection won't be complete, you'll be a lot better off inside the orbiter than outside."

Yukari was silent.

"Personally, I wouldn't recommend even doing a single full orbit. Discretion is definitely the better part of valor here. A brave astronaut is a dead astronaut. I'd like you both to consider what this risk means for you personally before deciding to go ahead with this."

"Thanks, Solomon. Over and out."

"Let me state for the record what I'd like to see," the captain said as soon as the transmission ended. "I don't like this plan. I'm grateful to both of you for your dedication and your passion, but I think you've done enough. Let's call it off."

"You're right..." Yukari said, the fire gone from her eyes.

She felt like she could do what had to be done in the space of two hours. But even if she made no mistakes herself, there was no telling what might happen up there. If they messed up their return timing for some reason, they might end up passing through the Van Allen belt more than once.

If I could just do it by myself without putting Akane at risk too...

Yukari turned to Akane. "Let's call this off. It's just not worth it."

Akane shook her head. "I appreciate what Satsuki said," she said. "But I think she's being too cautious. She's exaggerating the danger. I know it."

"I'm not too sure about that."

"The Apollo missions went through the Van Allen belts both ways. And they were up for days on the moon, which has no magnetic field at all. They must have endured a lot of radiation. And they were fine."

"But their equipment was designed for that, and let's face it, they were all old guys."

"We're hardly any different. Sexual development stops around the age of sixteen."

"Really...?"

Uh-oh. She's going to out-brain me here.

Yukari changed tack. "Well how do you *feel* about this? Are you confident we can do it?"

"Huh?"

"We had, what was it, four hours of sleep, and we've been working for fifteen hours straight. Do you think we can make it through the next seven hours without making a single mistake? Because that's what this is going to take."

A moment's hesitation passed over Akane's face. "Well, I've stayed up all night preparing for tests before—"

"Taking a test and navigating a spacecraft are two different things. And we'll need both of us working at full capacity in order to pull this off. If you made a mistake, it could mean both of our lives."

Akane's eyes fell, and Yukari immediately regretted her words. "I'm sorry, I take that back. I was only thinking of myself—"

Akane nodded and thought. For a full minute neither of the girls said anything.

Then Akane looked away and started to talk. "I know it's dangerous."

"Yeah."

"And I know Orpheus is just a machine."

"Yeah."

"But it's more than that. It's a dream...it's science! And I think it's worth risking my life for. I truly believe that," Akane said, her emotion spilling forth. "Yukari. We need to save Orpheus!"

At that moment, the whole mood on the middeck changed.

It was like all six of them there had signed the same unseen contract by some unspoken agreement.

We're not going home as failures. We can do this.

[ACT 11]

IN THE MANNED spacecraft design center located within the easternmost building on the Solomon base, a 3-D model of something resembling a bell was slowly rotating on a workstation screen.

The surface of the object was crisscrossed by a lattice-work of countless vectors, each square colored from white to red, purple, and blue. The object represented the orbiter *Mangosteen*, and the colors reflected surface temperatures at different points along a simulated reentry. A young technician was working the controls.

"Right, now increase impact speed by 640," Mukai, sitting off to the side, directed. The technician included the figure and restarted his simulation.

Once again, the simulated spaceship began to heat up. A separate window on the monitor showed a graph of peak temperatures.

"One thousand three hundred seventy...one thousand four hundred sixty...one thousand four hundred fifty... There's the peak."

"Huh? That low? That won't be a problem at all."

"Not in the model, at least," Mukai said.

Reentering the atmosphere from a height of three thousand kilometers was a first for an SSA orbiter. Falling from a greater height meant faster speeds. Greater speed meant more friction when the orbiter hit the atmosphere. Mukai had concerns that the orbiter wouldn't be able to take the heat.

Rough calculations had already shown it could, but as long as there was time left, it was his duty to keep running the numbers.

A maximum temperature of 1460° was lower than he had expected. Reentry speed had increased by a whole 10 percent, but their temperature hadn't climbed nearly as much.

It made him feel uneasy. "Try again with different parameters. Once they start on the rendezvous, we won't be able to stop them."

"Right."

Just then, the phone rang. Another technician answered. "Chief, it's the control center."

Mukai picked up the phone. "Right," he said then hung up. "Everyone, listen up. We just received word back from *Atlantis*. Operation: Rescue Orpheus is a go. We'll be here for another six hours, so everybody give it all you've got!"

A cheer rose up in the room. At the same time, things were

stirring at Johnson Space Center. George lit a cigar he kept for special occasions, stood up, and said, "All right, everybody! We're sending those girls up to meet Orpheus! Stay sharp and let's do this!"

[ACT 12]

"JUST GO TO sleep. Solomon will tell us everything we need to know."

"I just don't think you'll be able to do all the tying and the untying in those bulky suits..."

"We can do rope work when we need to."

The captain sent Yukari to her berth and closed the shade. "Sleep tight. I'll wake you up an hour before we start," he said from the other side.

Akane was nestled inside the berth below her. Though both of them resisted it at first, sleep came quickly.

In the payload bay, Norman and Gordon worked on securing *Mangosteen*. They had lowered the orbiter down to the floor of the bay, where they could use Kevlar fiber rope to attach it to the staging platform that had been installed to hold Orpheus.

Once the shuttle finished accelerating, they would have to release *Mangosteen* immediately. If they were late in cutting her loose, they would lose that much energy. Solomon had given them twenty seconds to pull the whole thing off.

In order to keep it tightly in place yet easily detachable, the brains at Johnson Space Center had settled on bow ties attached to three points. Instead of trying to make the ropes hold the orbiter in place during acceleration, they inserted a cushion between the orbiter and the platform beneath it to absorb the thrust. For the cushion they used an old Personal Rescue Enclosure—a large ball capable of holding a single astronaut in a fetal position for transport to a rescue shuttle—that was kept on the shuttle for unforeseen emergencies.

When they wanted to release *Mangosteen*, either Yukari or Akane would pull on those three ropes. Once they had undone the ties, they would jump in the orbiter and leave the shuttle behind.

"No, that's not how you do it," Norman said to Gordon. "Pass it through the loop from the bottom."

"Right, right. It's been a long time since Boy Scouts."

"You should go yachting. You learn this stuff whether you want to or not."

For maximum speed, they worked together, four hands helping to tie each knot.

"By the way," Gordon said, "I think Yukari wanted to tell you something."

"Probably remembered something else she wanted to say about how crappy I look in my space suit."

"That wasn't the impression I got."

"So what?" Norman snorted. "Let's get this thing tighter," he said, looking at the knot they were working on. "Don't want it coming undone during acceleration."

[ACT 13]

IT WAS AN hour before they began the rendezvous. The captain woke up Yukari and Akane. The girls used the vacuum toilet on the deck and wiped their faces and hands with a sponge. Then they put on their helmets and backpacks.

"How do you feel?"

"Couldn't be better."

"I can't believe I actually slept."

"That's good to hear." The captain passed a sheaf of fax papers bound with a ring to Yukari. "This is the latest procedural manual. Put it in this bag and keep it with you."

"Thanks."

Luis came down from the upper deck to see them off. "You two are the best," he said. "I hope we'll get to meet someday when we're back on the ground."

"I guess it depends on how this goes."

"It'll go fine," he said.

They shook hands, and Yukari and Akane went into the air lock. Outside, they found Norman and Gordon standing in front of *Mangosteen*, bathed in the glow from the giant blue arc of Earth toward the bow of the ship.

"Hi, Norman, Gordon," Yukari called to them on their intercoms, and the two men raised their arms to signal everything was ready. Together, both of them circled *Mangosteen*, checking the fastenings.

"This is tied down pretty well," Yukari said.

"All in a day's work," Norman replied.

"Okay, hand me the end of the rope."

"You won't be needing it."

"What?"

"You won't have time to pull the ropes, make sure the knots are undone, then get inside and close the hatch. Gordon and I will use knives to cut the lines instead."

"But Houston said they'd only give the okay on the condition that we handled the separation!"

"Houston doesn't need to know."

"That means we'll be accelerating the shuttle with both of you outside!"

"No worse than riding in a convertible. We'll be fine."

Yukari stared at the man's face behind his visor. She might as well have been looking at a mask.

"Well, this is a surprise," Yukari said, a smile playing on her lips. "I never knew NASA had such reckless pilots."

"Yukari!" Akane scolded.

"If you do something it's brave, but if we do the same thing, it's reckless. Is that it?"

"Norman, I should tell you," Akane said, "Yukari is completely incapable of directly expressing gratitude. Right, Yukari?"

"Right."

"See?"

Someone—maybe Gordon—blew a kind of bemused snort into his mic.

"Well, I'd certainly like to hear a word of gratitude now and then," Norman said. "The English word you're looking for begins with a *T*."

"Sorry, drawing a blank," Yukari said. "I'll be sure to let you know if I remember it. Let's go, Akane." Yukari moved to get into *Mangosteen*.

"I'm sorry. She's got this attitude—but she's really a good person inside," Akane said before turning to leave. Somehow, despite being entirely weightless, she managed to bow to the two NASA astronauts.

"Since when did you become my wife?" Yukari asked as soon as the cockpit pressurized.

"You haven't even apologized to him yet, Yukari! If you just thanked him, it would make that a lot easier, you know."

"It wasn't that I couldn't say it. I just want to say it without everyone listening in on the conversation."

"That just means you can't say it."

"What's the big deal, anyway?"

"I just think that with such an important task ahead of us, it's better to have none of these personal differences getting in the way."

"Really? I focus much better when I've got a little fight in me."

"Whatever works," Akane said. Now was no time for an argument.

Yukari fixed the procedural manual on top of the instrument panel and flipped on the communication switch. "*Atlantis*, this is *Mangosteen*. We're aboard. All systems are operational."

"Roger that, *Mangosteen*."

"Solomon, this is *Mangosteen*. Do you copy?"

"*Hoi*, *Mangosteen*. Loud and clear."

Together, the two girls read through their manual.

The rendezvous procedure would begin as they were flying over Midway Island, with Orpheus trailing two hundred kilometers behind them. They would slow down and let Orpheus catch up. Then, like the next runner in a relay race, they would accelerate to the same speed to match Orpheus as it approached.

First, *Atlantis* would fire its orbital maneuvering system engine for six minutes on full thrust.

As soon as the burn finished, they would detach *Mangosteen* within twenty seconds and say farewell.

Then *Mangosteen* would fire its OMS engine for five minutes on full thrust.

This burn had to wait until they were clear of *Atlantis*, so Yukari would start the sequence by hand. The computer would take over after that.

Once both craft had finished their burns, eleven minutes would pass until *Mangosteen* and *Orpheus* were flying side-by-side far above the Hawaiian Islands.

Four minutes later, Solomon would remotely adjust *Mangosteen*'s orbit after pinpointing the locations one final time. If a fuel check at that point showed insufficient reserves, the mission would be scrubbed. Nineteen minutes total would have passed by the time the orbit adjustment was complete. Then Yukari would nudge the orbiter as close as possible to Orpheus while Akane went outside to remove the wire shorting out Orpheus's engine control and pull the safety tag.

Ideally, all of this had to happen in the space of twenty minutes. At that point they would be over two thousand kilometers up, and the radiation would only get worse.

Forty minutes after the rendezvous procedure had begun, they would get back inside the orbiter in the sky over Brazil. Twenty minutes later, they would reach their apogee at an altitude of three thousand kilometers while passing over southern Africa.

Here, they would fire a short retrograde burn and leave orbit. Orpheus would remain above them, ready to fire its upper-stage engine as it passed over Indonesia and leave Earth's gravitational pull altogether.

Around the same time, *Mangosteen* would reenter the atmosphere just east of Japan, doing a half orbit of the earth to splashdown off the coast of Chile. U.S. Navy helicopters would be waiting near the splashdown zone to shuttle the two of them back to a carrier.

"Wait a second—what's this all about?" Yukari read out one of the warnings written in her manual. "'While Akane is outside the craft, take *Mangosteen* to a safe distance.'"

"A precaution in case the engines fire. I guess they'd rather save one of us than none of us."

"That is *so* not cool."

"No, it's okay. If it did fire, you wouldn't have any fuel to chase after me anyway." Akane giggled nervously. "Believe me—I'd be happy to go to Pluto."

"Great. My copilot is a space kamikaze."

"I think we all have to be, at least a little bit. I knew that when I applied for the job."

She's tougher than she seems, Yukari thought. *Time to pull it together.*

"Well, I'm not retreating to a safe distance, and that's that," Yukari said. "Keep your lifeline tied on. The second you think something might be going wrong, push away from Orpheus. Don't let that propulsion exhaust get you."

"But, Yukari—"

"That's an order from your captain!"

Time marched relentlessly on. Houston was in charge of watching the clock and counting off the seconds.

"Orpheus is approaching two hundred thirty climbers behind you. *Atlantis*, you have fifty seconds until OMS burn."

"All systems are ready," Berkheimer confirmed from the shuttle.

"*Atlantis*, thirty seconds until OMS burn."

"We're ready to fire. Norman, Gordon, you two sitting down out there?"

"You bet we're sitting."

"*Atlantis*, start your sequence. Ignition in ten seconds...four... three...two...ignition."

A jolt passed through the shuttle, and they felt a gentle weight pressing on their backs.

"Houston, this is *Atlantis*. We have a confirmed OMS burn."

"This is *Mangosteen*. No unusual vibration in here."

"Roger that. Orpheus is approaching the hundred-seventy-kilometer mark. Three minutes forty-five seconds until separation."

The sound of the engines firing was barely audible through the ship vibrations, despite the fact that seven tons of force were being generated just a few meters away.

"Norman, Gordon, you still sitting down?"

"We're both doing great."

"*Atlantis*, *Mangosteen*. One minute until burn completion."

I wonder what they're up to?

Yukari took a look through the periscope, but something was in the way, and she couldn't see the two NASA astronauts outside. If she said anything to them now, *Atlantis* and the entire space communications network would hear. But there was no guarantee that they would be able to communicate at all after separation.

Yukari bit her lip.

I waited too long, and now I missed my moment.

"*Atlantis* and *Mangosteen*. Twenty seconds until burn completion."

"Houston, this is *Mangosteen*. We are ready to fire engines. All systems are go." Yukari lifted the cover on the sequencer activation switch and held her finger over it.

"All crew prepare for weightlessness. I'll count it down. Weightlessness in five…four…three…one…complete burn now, begin separation!"

"The lines are free," Norman said almost immediately. "*Atlantis*, begin evasive maneuvers."

In the periscope protruding from the bottom of the orbiter, Yukari saw the payload bay drop away into the distance. Then she saw the two wings, the engine housing, the nose—the entire shuttle—drifting away, becoming lost in the giant blue sphere of the earth.

"Separation complete. *Mangosteen*, begin!"

Yukari pressed the activation switch.

This time, the sound of the engine was a roar, the vibrations more intense.

That's more like it.

"This is *Mangosteen*. Sequence started. OMS firing. Everything's looking good." Yukari kept her finger on the talk button. "Norman, Gordon, Luis, Captain Berkheimer, thank you all. And I'm sorry about earlier. You're the bravest, coolest people I know. We'll try not to let you down."

Akane's eyes opened wide.

Yukari stared at the instrument panel, muttering to herself. "I can't believe I said it. Must be the adrenaline."

[ACT 14]

A PHONE CALL came into the control center for Mukai.

"What? What? Just calm down. Tell me everything in order."

Whoever was on the other end, they were panicking.

"What? The Cdb settings...three whole steps! What about max temperature? Sixteen hundred seventy degrees? Are you kidding me?" The color drained from Mukai's face.

"What is it?" Kinoshita asked.

"Our atmospheric resistance coefficients were off—er, that is—"

"Bottom line, please."

"If *Mangosteen* reenters the atmosphere at its currently predicted speed, it's going to disintegrate."

"For real?"

Every controller within earshot turned around.

"They ran it through simulations on three models—apparently the bad numbers in the constant database came from a copy/paste error. I'm sorry, this is my fault!"

"*Hoi?* Did someone say disintegration?" Matsuri asked.

"Say nothing to those two up there," Kinoshita told her quickly. "*Hoi...*"

"What do we do?" Mukai wailed, his mouth twisting. "They're nearly entirely out of fuel—"

"The *first* thing we do," Kinoshita said, "is calm down. They're already in their orbit. We can't change that now. We have to proceed with the mission as planned and use what time remains to figure out a way to get them back through the atmosphere safely. This is on us now."

"We've already determined optimal reentry path, and it's disastrous."

"What's going on? Something wrong?" Nasuda had noticed the commotion on the floor and come out of the observation room.

Kinoshita explained the situation, but Nasuda did not appear particularly moved. "I see," was all he said. While outspoken when it was time to celebrate, Nasuda kept all other emotions in check. "What if we pulled them up a little, had them come in shallower."

"That won't work. They'd just bounce off the atmosphere and come back at an even steeper angle."

"Any chance of stealing fuel from Orpheus? It's using hydrazine too, isn't it?"

"Well—"

"Impossible," Kinoshita said. "The tank on Orpheus is semipermanently sealed due to the long distance it has to travel."

Nasuda grunted and thought for a while before saying, "I don't want them to know about this yet. Tell Houston everything. They're going to have to beef up the recovery team."

[ACT 15]

THE ORBITAL CORRECTION went perfectly. Orpheus was only fifteen meters ahead of them now. The cylindrical shape of its upper-stage engine glittered against a backdrop of inky darkness.

They had already evacuated the air from the orbiter in preparation for Akane's spacewalk. Akane strapped on a waist pouch to carry the tools she would need. This time, there would be no need to strip off her backpack and crawl inside anything. Both the safety tag and jumper wire were easily accessible by hand from the outside.

Yukari gave the engine a few more bursts, trying to close the distance as quickly as possible without wasting any fuel.

"Ten meters to Orpheus. Akane's just opened the hatch."

"*Hoi.* Good luck, you two." Matsuri's voice was flat.

"Here I go," Akane said.

"Be careful."

Akane opened up the hatch on the right side of the orbiter and poked her head outside.

Meanwhile, Yukari opened the hatch on the left to get a better view of the operation. Orpheus's upper-stage engine hung in space directly in front of them.

Yukari checked the countdown on her watch.

Twenty-seven minutes into the rendezvous. So far, so good.

"Want me to lower the nose?"

"Yes, please—I'm off."

Akane lightly kicked her seat and drifted outside. Her lifeline twisted and coiled behind her like a living thing. Within moments, she was grabbing onto the cover over Orpheus's engine, working her way up to the upper lip.

Yukari glanced down at the diagram in her manual. "About fifty centimeters to your right. That's it. Right there."

"Yep." Akane stuck her helmet over the edge and looked inside. "There it is. I've spotted the jumper wire. One end of it has come loose. It's just floating there."

"Be careful not to touch anything around it."

"Roger that."

Akane pulled a small pair of wire clippers from her waist pouch and stuck them inside. "I've cut the wire."

Yukari breathed a sigh of relief.

"Next up is the safety tag...and it's out."

"You did it! That was quick!"

"Easier done than said, I guess," Akane said, laughter in her voice.

"Houston, this is *Mangosteen*. Akane has just succeeded in removing the jumper wire and the safety tag."

"Great job, *Mangosteen*! We've just confirmed it with our telemetry. Can you hear the commotion down here? I haven't heard this much cheering in a long time."

The signal was so weak they could barely hear the controller's voice, let alone any cheering.

Akane followed her lifeline back to the orbiter. Yukari grabbed onto her ankle and began pulling her inside, when Akane stopped. She had just turned around for the first time.

"Wait! Just a second—"

"What?"

"It's amazing, Yukari. Come look—"

Yukari wanted to close the hatch quickly before they got any higher, but something in Akane's voice made her undo her harness and pull herself up to the hatch rim.

She stuck her torso out and turned to face the stern of the orbiter.

Yukari was stunned. She had never seen the earth like this.

They were over two thousand kilometers away now, as far away as if you took the entire Japanese archipelago and stood it on its end pointing straight up. From this height, the horizon formed a perfect circle.

Directly beneath them, the Amazon River snaked through a thick green canopy. To the north was Cuba, the Gulf of Mexico, and the Florida peninsula—she could even see as far as Washington D.C. and New York, hazy in the atmosphere.

To the south, she could see most of the South American continent, bordered by the vast expanses of the Pacific and Atlantic Oceans— she could even see further south, to the point where the oceans met.

Cirrus clouds wove serpentine paths through the sky below, following the currents of the jet stream. A hurricane gathered strength toward the middle latitudes. Lightning flashed in the valleys formed by towering cumulonimbus clouds. Then she noticed the creeping hemisphere of night, coming in from the east.

"It's evening in the Sahara right now," Akane said. "That's the sunset, right there. That line. That's what it really means."

"Yeah…" Yukari stared, lost in the view. Akane grabbed her wrist. She was facing Yukari now.

"Thank you."

"Huh?"

"Thank you for bringing me up here. Thank you, Yukari."

"Akane, you came here on your own—hey!" Yukari waved her hands. "No crying! Stop it!" She laughed. "Cry in your suit and you won't be able to see a thing."

"Ack, you're right," Akane said. "I forgot I can't wipe my eyes with my helmet on."

"Let's go. We really need to get inside."

"Yeah."

The two girls made their way inside the orbiter and shut the hatch.

"Solomon, this is *Mangosteen*. We're back inside. The earth is incredible from up here. So, time to go diving off Chile."

"*Hoi*. Congratulations, you two."

"Huh? What's up, Matsuri? That's the least cheerful-sounding congratulations I've ever heard."

A few moments passed before Matsuri answered. "Yukari, Akane, I have something really important to tell you."

"What?"

"I snuck in a rambutan fruit under your life raft. I want you both to eat it. It'll help ward away evil spirits and bring good luck. Okay?"

"What? You smuggled fruit in here again?"

"You have to eat it, both of you. Promise?"

"Well, okay, but why are you telling us this on an open channel?"

"Please. It'll keep you safe."

For the first time, Yukari realized something wasn't right. "Safe from what, Matsuri? Is something up?"

"I'll tell you once you're done eating."

[ACT 16]

THE CHEERING HADN'T lasted long in the mission control room at Johnson Space Center. They'd just received the update from Solomon. The two girls, barely sixteen years old, were going to die. The mood on the floor was one of despair.

So this is what you get when you take a risk, thought George. *In the end, someone always pays.*

Except not with the *Apollo* 13. The crew then had returned alive, miraculously. What George needed now was another miracle. Just then, a flash of inspiration shot across the back of George's mind. He stood up and shouted, "What y'all need is some good old-fashioned optimism! This is just like coming back from the moon, people. We've been through this before, thirty years ago!"

The chief of flight dynamics in the seat in front of him looked back. "What are you going on about?"

"I'm talking about a double-dip reentry! You make the nose of the orbiter go up and down as she's just entering the atmosphere to kill speed!"

When the *Apollo* spacecraft returned from the moon, they were going at a much faster speed than the shuttle. If they went straight in they'd burn up, so instead, they popped in and out of the atmosphere like a jumping dolphin, shaving off velocity with every bob.

"But how can *Mangosteen* control the orientation of its nose?"

"Don't tell me you forgot, Randall! Capsules can generate lift, too—and if they change their attitude, they can change the amount of that lift. The *Apollo* did it with attitude control thrusters."

"You're right...wait—" A light came on in Randall's eyes. "We've got *Mangosteen*'s data here. We just need to know her center of gravity and her front profile. I think I can use the data from the *Apollo* modules to figure it out from there."

"Then get on it. Those girls saved our asses, now it's our turn to save theirs!"

George contacted Solomon. "This is Houston. I've got a question. Is *Mangosteen* capable of adjusting its attitude during reentry?"

It was Kinoshita who answered. "Not through the usual means, no. Why?"

"If we can adjust her angle even slightly, we should be able to use a partial skip reentry to reduce the temperature levels. I'm calculating a flight path now."

"Like *Apollo*, of course! Even that was never tried, but it should work."

"Glad you studied our methods. But if they can't control their attitude coming in, it's not going to do us much good. Can you think of any way to pull this off?"

"Well, you can't use the sequencer to fire the attitude thrusters during reentry, and we can't use remote control. Manual control might do it—but at high G, that's not going to be easy."

"Where's the control stick located?"

"Just in front of the right armrest."

"Like a jet fighter, right. That just might be doable—it's worth a try, isn't it?"

"You get a hardened, strong fighter pilot up there, maybe...not that we have any other choice. Give me your results as soon as you have them. We'll owe you a big one if this works."

"We're on it." George turned to Randall. "How soon?"

"Give me five minutes."

"Make it three." He turned back to the phone. "Mr. Kinoshita? We'll have it for you in five minutes."

[ACT 17]

"WHAT? WHAT PROBLEM on reentry? Out with it, Matsuri!"

"*Hoi hoi*, Yukari, I will, it's just I'm not totally sure what the problem is myself yet. Hang on a second. I'll put Kinoshita on."

"I need you both to stay calm and listen up," Kinoshita told them as soon as he was on the mic. "Sorry to put this on you now, but if we allow you to proceed on your planned course, there's a chance you could disintegrate on reentry."

"What?" Akane yelped.

"You've gotta be kidding me!"

"Curse me all you want, but save it for later. We made a mistake, basically, but there's a way out of this. We're going to have you adjust your attitude on reentry to avoid overheating."

"Adjust during reentry? Uh, is that even possible?"

"Yes, but you'll have to do it yourself, manually. Time to flex those arm muscles, Yukari."

"Flex my...what? You want me to pilot this thing at 8 G?"

"Preferably you'll be finished with your maneuvers before the Gs get that bad. Around 5 or 6 G."

"That's still asking a lot of a dainty little girl, Kinoshita."

"All we have up there is dainty little girls, if I'm not mistaken. So one of you has to do this."

"You have a point. So what do I do, exactly?"

"You'll be bringing the nose of the orbiter up and down three times. The trick is in the timing and the angle. You'll need to maintain the right angle for the right amount of time and know when to switch. NASA's just sent us the numbers. There are twenty-four time/angle checkpoints for you to keep track of."

"You're going to read them off to me, right? There's no way I can remember that many."

"No, actually. Remember we can't talk on the radio during reentry.

You'll have to write it down and stick it on your instrument panel."

"Okay. Let me get some paper." Yukari opened the procedure manual to the blank pages at the end. "Hey, Akane, can I borrow a pen? I gave mine to Luis."

"What, you too?"

"No way. He got your pen?"

"Yeah…he said it would be a good souvenir."

"Does that guy have a souvenir obsession or what? Tell me we have an extra pen somewhere."

Akane shook her head. "You think they'd stow extras of *anything* in an SSA orbiter?"

"So what do we do? Carve it in something with a knife?"

"You'd never be able to read it with all the turbulence. It's hard enough to see the instruments."

"We could cut our fingers and write it in blood?"

"The numbers'd be too big. We don't have enough paper. And we don't have time for that anyway."

"Kinoshita?" Yukari said. "You're not going to believe this, but we have nothing to write with up here. Any ideas?"

"Well," Akane cut in, "I could memorize them and read them off to you."

"What, all those numbers?"

"It's forty-eight numbers in all, right? That shouldn't be a problem. I'm pretty good at remembering things."

"You sure you can do that, Akane?"

"Just read them off to me slowly. I'll do my best."

"Right, here goes." Kinoshita began reading off the list.

Akane closed her eyes and tapped her forehead with a finger once for every number. When he was finished, Akane read them back.

"Perfect! That's incredible!" Kinoshita was practically cheering.

"Way to go, grade-A student!"

"Okay, now that that's taken care of, proceed with your scheduled course—just be careful not to waste a drop of fuel.

You've got twenty-one minutes left till reentry."

Of course, had anyone thought it through, there was a serious flaw with this plan. With all the intelligent people on the ground and up in orbit, you'd think someone would have realized it, and yet mistakes like this happen all the time in spaceflight operations. Like a magician's sleight of hand, it was right there in front of Kinoshita's face and he never saw it coming.

Two hours had passed since the rendezvous began. *Mangosteen* made a full circuit before dropping from orbit fifteen hundred kilometers to the east of the Ogasawara Islands, out in the Pacific to the southwest of Tokyo.

Though the Gs were still relatively light, they could hear the sound of friction on the hull growing steadily louder.

"It's starting, Akane."

"Yeah..."

"Well, once again a whole lot happened, but in the end, it worked out. Right?"

"We did save Orpheus, at least."

"Hey, we did a great job! Everyone did. I was impressed with you, Akane. You're a full-fledged astronaut already."

"Really? Th-thanks." Akane's cheeks blushed pink.

That's my girl, Yukari thought proudly.

The vibrations increased and the light outside the window was tinged with orange. They were back in gravity now. One G...2 G... 3 G...

Yukari grabbed the control stick with her right hand, then placed her left hand over it. *I can do this. If I use my other wrist to hold my hand up, I can maintain control.*

"Akane, checkpoint one?"

No answer.

"Akane, checkpoint numbers please!"

Akane said nothing.

"Hey, Akane...no way!" Yukari could practically hear the blood drain from her face. Akane had lost consciousness the moment the G began to rise, just as she had on takeoff. "Yo! Akane! Don't do this to me! Wake up, Akane! Wake up! What do I do? What angle? Hey! Heeey!"

Yukari couldn't even lift her arm to nudge Akane by that point. She screamed. "Fine! I'll just do it by instinct! Hey, as long as we're alive, who cares where we land!"

All she could remember was that she had to raise the nose and lower it three times. She pulled up and instantly felt like she'd left the atmosphere, but the G picked right up again. When she felt like she might not be able to take any more, she changed the angle again, and the G dropped off. Akane still wasn't waking up. The G began to climb again. Up, down, up, down. It was like a never-ending nightmare.

Yukari's arms felt leaden with fatigue. She couldn't feel anything in her fingers, and everything looked blurry.

Enough...I've done enough, right? That's all I have to do...right? You can give me that medal now...I'm ready.

It's all up to you now, Mangosteen. *Just don't forget to open that parachute.*

Yukari gave up trying. Her hands let go of the control stick.

And she slept.

"...Unidentified aircraft, this is Tokyo Control. Please respond. Aircraft of unidentified origin flying over the Sea of Japan, respond immediately."

Yukari's eyes fluttered open.

Huh? What happened? Did we make it...?

All she could see through the porthole was blue sky.

"Aircraft of unidentified origin flying over the Sea of Japan, this is Tokyo Control. Please respond immediately."

Tokyo Control? Did we make another half orbit during reentry?

"Uh, hey, Tokyo Control! This is the spacecraft *Mangosteen.*

We read you."

"Space…what!? You again? Yukari?"

"Er, yeah, it's me. Sorry to bother you again like this."

"What's your current altitude, *Mangosteen*? And destination, if you even know."

"We're at twenty-two kilometers or so. Our splashdown target *was* in the South Pacific, but…"

"Roger that. We'll play it just like last time."

"I think that's wise, yes."

"We'll give the police and the fire department and the coast guard and the Self-Defense Force the heads up."

"Thanks for that. Any idea where it looks like we're falling this time?"

"You're on pretty much the same course you were on last time, actually. Heading for Kanagawa, maybe Tokyo Harbor or Sagami."

"Again?"

"That's how it looks from here."

There was a jolt as the orbiter's parachute opened.

"How could we possibly be landing in the same place?" Yukari wondered aloud. "Don't tell me we're going to hit Nellis again. That would be too much." She shook her head. "No, that's not happening. That curse was a one-time deal. I'm through with that."

She switched from the fuel cells to the shielded batteries and purged O_2 and H_2.

Life support systems, off.

External ventilation activated.

She checked the periscope.

Yokohama.

With a tremendous *woosh!* of water, *Mangosteen* landed.

"Akane! Wake up! We're here! I don't know where here is, but we're here!"

"Hunh…Yukari? What? We're back? Did we land in water?"

"We did. I'm not entirely sure it's the ocean, but we definitely hit water."

"Wow."

Is that all you have to say? Yukari thought as she undid her harness and opened the hatch. The first thing she saw was a small sign that read: THE DRAGONFLIES THANK YOU FOR KEEPING OUR POND CLEAN!

That's it. Nothing will ever surprise me again. If some supernatural force is going through all this trouble to play an elaborate joke on me, I surrender. Why fight it?

"Akane?" Yukari closed the hatch. "If you're sick of this whole astronaut thing, now's your chance to go back to school."

"No thanks." Her cheeks were still blushing—lingering excitement from just before she had passed out. "I think I know where I need to be to learn. I need to be in space."

It was a grade-A student sort of thing to say. She was ready to keep going, even though she had passed out both on takeoff and reentry.

"All students return to your classrooms immediately!"

The clamor outside was growing louder.

Not the principal again. Wait, what was it Matsuri said?

"You know someone else who would want to curse that school?"

Someone else...

Yukari's eyes darted over to Akane.

"You didn't!"

"Didn't what?"

"You cursed Nellis Academy!"

"What? That's ridiculous. I didn't curse any—" Akane's mouth clapped shut mid-sentence. A single bead of sweat formed on her forehead. "I don't curse. I just don't."

"You sure about that?"

Yukari stared at the other girl. Akane just sat there, sweat rolling down her face.

AFTERWORD

WHEN THIS BOOK was first published in 1996, it was to praise very unusual for one of my books. "I cried!" "I fell in love!" the starry-eyed critics said—so of course it sold out everywhere and became one of those books everyone knows yet no one's read because they couldn't find it. As this is that book (not to mention part of the story covered in the anime version of *Rocket Girls*), if you're reading this in a bookstore right now, now's your chance. Opportunity only knocks once, and all that.

I tend to use my afterwords for shameless self-promotion and sales pitches, and this one's no exception, so here goes!

In this book, we meet the third Rocket Girl, Akane Miura. A genius who can model difficult orbits with a simple calculator, yet shy, almost reclusive—a delicate flower in all the right ways. If this were *Sailor Moon*, she might be Sailor Mercury. Kind of an old reference, I know, but the point is she's a good kid and she's cute.

Let's take a look at our three Rocket Girls through the lens of dialogue, shall we? Akane's what we call an *otaku*—which is basically anyone obsessed with something. You might say nerd. Usually she doesn't talk much at all, but get her going on one of her pet topics and watch out! Meanwhile, Yukari's the type who *has* to talk if someone else is there, or she can't relax. Matsuri's cheerful but not a big talker. She can be with a friend and say nothing at all. An enjoy-the-silence type. That's my take on them at least. Your results may vary.

I'd like to talk about the bit toward the end of the book, where they're attempting to salvage a probe mission to Pluto gone awry.

On August 24, 2006, the International Astronomical Union redefined what exactly a planet was, and Pluto was dropped from the list. Of course, the line in my book where I say "Pluto isn't as exciting as the other planets" is forever trapped on the other side of this historical divide. When reprints of this book came out, I considered amending the section, but ultimately decided not to. Pluto, as portrayed in this book, was based on the current knowledge at the time the book was written. Even now, the feel of Pluto is the same—the only thing that's changed is the words.

At the time of writing, astronomy fans knew that Pluto was on its way out, based on the changing definition of a planet, but it took IAU over ten years to officially make the change. I present this book as a historical document of that time in limbo.

In fact, the NASA probe New Horizons is currently on its way to Pluto, the Kuiper belt object. It's the fastest probe we've ever sent out, and it's still going to take until August 2015 for it to reach Pluto. It's a long trip, but to the people who dreamed it and made it happen, every day is worth it.

I hope this book lets you share, even a little, in their joy.

Housuke Nojiri
November 2006

ABOUT THE AUTHOR

Born in Mie, Japan, in 1961. After working in instrumentation control, CAD programming, and game design, Housuke Nojiri published his first work, *The Blind Spot of Veis*, based on the video game *Creguian*, in 1992. He gained popularity with his subsequent works the *Creguian* series and the *Rocket Girls* series. In 2002, he published *Usurper of the Sun*, ushering in a new era of space science fiction in Japan. After first appearing as a series of short stories, *Usurper* won the Seiun Award for best Japanese science fiction novel of 2002 and was published in English in 2009. His other works include *Pendulum of Pinieru* and *Fuwa-Fuwa no Izumi*.

HAIKASORU
THE FUTURE IS JAPANESE

MARDOCK SCRAMBLE BY TOW UBUKATA

Why me? It was to be the last thought a young prostitute, Rune-Balot, would ever have... as a human anyway. Taken in by a devious gambler named Shell, she became a slave to his cruel desires and would have been killed by his hand if not for the self-aware All-Purpose Tool (and little yellow mouse) known as Oeufcoque. Now a cyborg, Balot is not only nigh-invulnerable but has the ability to disrupt electrical systems of all sorts. But even these powers may not be enough for Balot to deal with Shell, who offloads his memories to remain above the law, the immense assassin Dimsdale-Boiled, or the neon-noir streets of Mardock City itself.

MIRROR SWORD AND SHADOW PRINCE BY NORIKO OGIWARA

When the heir to the empire comes to Mino, the lives of young Oguna and Toko change forever. Oguna is drafted to become a *shadow* prince, a double trained to take the place of the hunted royal. But soon Oguna is given the Dragon Sword, and his ability to wield it threatens the entire nation. Only Toko can stop him, but to do so she needs to gather four magatama, beads with magical powers that can be strung together to form the Misumaru of death. Toko's journey is one of both adventure and self-discovery, and also brings her face to face with the tragic truth behind Oguna's transformation. A story of two parallel quests, of a pure love tried by the power of fate, the second volume of Tales of the Magatama is as thrilling as *Dragon Sword and Wind Child*.

GOOD LUCK, YUKIKAZE BY CHŌHEI KAMBAYASHI

The alien JAM have been at war with humanity for over thirty years...or have they? Rei Fukai of the FAF's Special Air Force and his intelligent tactical reconnaissance fighter plane Yukikaze have seen endless battles, but after declaring "Humans are unnecessary now," and forcibly ejecting Fukai, Yukikaze is on its own. Is the target of the JAM's hostility really Earth's machines? And have the artificial intelligences of Earth been acting in concert with the JAM from the start to manipulate Yukikaze? As Rei tries to discover the truth behind the intentions of both sides, he realizes that his own humanity may be at risk, and that the JAM are about to make themselves known to the world at large.

And also by **HOUSUKE NOJIRI**

ROCKET GIRLS

Yukari Morita is a high school girl on a quest to find her missing father. While searching for him in the Solomon Islands, she receives the offer of a lifetime— she'll get the help she needs to find her father and all she need do in return is become the world's youngest, lightest astronaut. Yukari and her sister Matsuri, both petite, are the perfect crew for the Solomon Space Association's launches, or will be once they complete their rigorous and sometimes dangerous training.

VISIT US AT WWW.HAIKASORU.COM